Magnus and Prime:
Stone Soul

A Fantasy Novel

By Jack Robinson

This is Paperback Edition 2020

First Edition

Printed by Kindle Publishing 2020

Copyright © Jack Robinson 2020

ISBN 978-1-9996060-8-4

New Beginnings: A Foreword

I believe that there's always time and chance to start anew. If something got off on the wrong foot, then there's no shame in starting again. This ideal is what birthed Stone Soul.

I'm not one for removing or deleting content, so this book isn't meant to remove Meeting of the Minds: Volume 1 from existence. However, as you'll soon find out, Stone Soul is a great way to dip a toe into the pool of fantastic literature that is Magnus and Prime.

To clarify, after reading this book the next one to read is MotM: Volume 1. This story just helps grant new readers a smoother start to the series, and older fans a chance to visit some of our favourite characters prior to the events of Volume 1. A prequel of sorts.

I hope you enjoy, and I'll see you in the next Volume… whichever one that may be for you. Have fun, and keep on being awesome.

Map of Valordolt

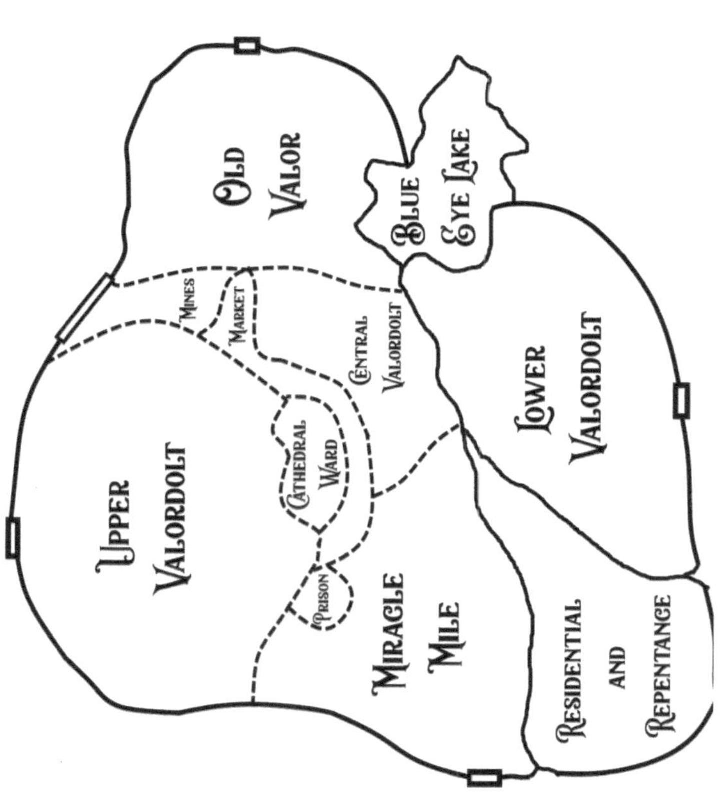

Table of Contents

Magnus and Prime:
Stone Soul

By Jack Robinson

By Jack Robinson

<u>Prologue</u>

Hericore never felt safe in his own skin. Fate had woven him a faulty tapestry from birth, not a single thread stitched with grace or love. Whatever god above had sown his seed must've been absent of care, of mind, or of both.

It wasn't disdain or malice that made him the person he was. It was neglect, and negligence stung far more than hatred.

However, not one to be defeated by fate, he pushed forward in life. The gods of Prime were weak, and it was this weakness that drew Hericore to them. He didn't want a better fortune, he wanted a better future. Once one hard-fought victory struck him, and it rolled into the next. Eventually, the ill-fated fool was seated as ambassador to the gods, or *a* god, at least.

'Arch-Paladin of the Order,' that was his title now. A hollow holding, void of any real achievement. The Order worshipped a golden goddess of health and vitality, yet everything and everyone beneath their object of sanctity was anything but. The Vitalands they protected were ravaged by corruption, both physical and political. They ruled a cancerous land, and eventually that cancer had spread to Hericore's very being.

Over the months his health had slipped, and with the fall that followed came a string of horrid symptoms. His hands shook and writhed with thick ravines of pus cutting deep to the bone. His eyes would spasm and roll back and forth at even the faintest light on the dullest days.

Worst of all was the bouts of breathlessness that gave every word he spoke a lingering wheeze. Nothing was more terrifying than the fear of each breath being his last. Death was coming, but it was what awaited behind the veil of fatality that scared the aged Arch-Paladin.

Time was fleeting for him – so fleeting that something needed to be done. Yet no one under the Order's banner sought to fight for him, save for a handful of equally ill-fated failures. One such failure was standing before him now.

"Philip." Hericore spoke through raspy cords. "Is it time?"

In his old age Hericore required an assistant, a spirit of vigour that could wave away the notion that the old man was on death's door. A semblance of youth to flavour the grey gruel of decay.

The plucky boy was barely through adulthood's door, and yet he held near infinite potential. All young ones did, but Philip was so much more. He was ambition, he was charisma, he was… a little bit of an ass.

Looking down at a bronze watch, engraved with ancient text, Philip smirked and confirmed, "Visitation has begun, boss man."

It was no secret that the boy's watch hadn't ticked a tock in years, but flair meant much to the wannabe wise man. Who was Hericore to deny him a little fun?

"Good. Eyes on the exits, if you would. They will prove useful… some day." Hericore passed Philip, the spirit of vigour himself, and pressed onward to deal with spirits of a whole other kind. "Oh, no touching the Warden's walls this time. The rumours of gold within the prison are likely just lies of the layman."

With an unassuming grin and a wink, Philip said, "Gotcha. I'll keep my beak clean." As Hericore started his pained stagger up a stretch of stairs, he heard a whisper slip from the ground level. "One of us has to."

Dismissing the foolish boy to his hopeless pursuits, they parted ways before Hericore arrived atop the stairs and across from a whole new breed of hopeless. The type of hope extinguished unwillingly in the iron grip of 'justice.'

A corridor apart stood the two. One was the head of the Order, the other was subject to life's unending chaos. It was in these dank and dreary walls that they were destined to meet. A parley had been granted by the warden of this palace of peril, and all that reside within it.

It was a bland block of blackness with an even blander purpose, to capture and leash the criminals of the corrupted Vitalands. Central Block, it was called; one part of three that made up the Order's biggest prison. A fancy grave to bury the darkest minds of the land, far from the bright eyes of the common folk.

Warding over the oily dimness of Central Block was a man of little character, or none that he would allow you to glean. He was a monster in his own right, one big enough to rule over all the others. A grey-face of solemn expression sat above a statuesque body, tightly squeezed into a suit that didn't suit him.

By Jack Robinson

The Warden did nothing and simply gestured at the
end of the corridor, towards the failure who was
attempting to flail about the place. A prisoner, older
than most around him and longer serving than them
all. He was bound to a chair of small spikes, worn from
years of use, and blinded and gagged by the same
length of rag. A man given less respect than an animal.

Screaming through his rags, the prisoner was
mumbling out a fearful cry. This was profound for
many reasons, most due to the fact this one criminal
had been mute for years, maybe decades. For a spark to
ignite him now meant a great change was coming, one
sensed in the old bones of a mildly-maddened man.

"The mad dog barks again," seethed the Warden
with a chilling tone. "Claims there are ghosts roaming
the place. I think he's clearly gone mad. But, Order rule
states the Arch-Paladin must sign off on this incident. If
there's really spectral pests about, we'll need to bust
'em. Either that or give me the signal to put this mutt
down."

Typical of the Warden to treat spirits of the damned
as common vermin and to call for the death of a
panicked prisoner. Stories of the Warden's past with

certain prisoners was well known, and this particular prisoner was special to him.

"There will be no murder today, Percival," ordered Hericore. "I wish to have a moment with the prisoner. Alone."

Begrudgingly, the Warden let this be and without further remark he skulked back to his office. Hericore's job was now simple: silence the prisoner's screams and listen to his words. Before the Warden vanished completely, Hericore asked him one last thing. "What's his name?"

"It's mud. That's all you need to know," replied the Warden as he slammed his door tightly shut.

Ignoring the ignorance of the brutish response, Hericore marched forth. He passed the other high-security cells and the pair of black-iron guards before the prisoner's cell. The Arch-Paladin held no fear and pressed on in confidence.

The small and tight walls of the prison scraped against the top of his head as he cut a brisk pace into the cell. With a door slam of his own, he sealed off the outside world and managed to find a modicum of peace without it. Only the gentle raindrops of a spring dawn could be heard from outside. Serenity cradled the cruelty within both men and their hearts.

"Grinning ghost," repeated the prisoner. "G-grinning ghost."

Placing a firm palm on the prisoner's hand, Hericore felt every bump and bruise on the man's bony flesh. Along the forearm were needle marks from failed medicinal ends to tonight's conflict. Beatings and narcotics would get them nowhere – this task required something far more gentle.

Keeping a grasp on the prisoner's arm, Hericore stood over him and whispered softly into his ear, "Good morning, Kenneth. This place may seem like hell on Magnus, but hold tight just a little longer."

The man immediately ceased his cries and snapped to attention. All fear and worry halted as a wave of realisation hit him: the feeling of salvation, one that cut to his core and stretched back as far as he could remember.

After the decrepit paladin removed his gag, the equally decrepit prisoner replied, "Who are you?"

With a small smile on his sickly face, the sly Arch-Paladin said, "My name is Hericore, and I'm going to set you free."

By Jack Robinson

Chapter 1: Eleventh Hour

Ish was old, but never wiser. Ish had a kindly warmth, but he'd never experienced that of another. Ish was tired, but he could never seem to sleep.

Time was lost to the clockmaker, each 'tick' indistinguishable from the following 'tock'. If enough time was spent on an art it's no longer an art, but a part of one's self. Giving a lifetime to the inner workings of machines made Ish's very mind run like clockwork.

A short man, wrinkled, and far from stout, he resembled a malnourished turkey in sight and stature – even owning a similarly saggy neck. Wearing a navy cardigan and grey slacks, his attire contradicted the gruelling expression he wore. It was a look forged by cold weather rather than the turmoil of work. Loving life on all fronts – save for the horrid weather – made Ish's sour expression a guilt-ridden one. He smiled where he could and apologised when he could not.

The most notable thing about Ish was a bushy moustache that stuck out from his grey, balding head. This 'stache was free to grow, and in return warmed his upper lips in the coldness. Above the thick lip warmer sat a pair of spectacles; also thick, but gold at the rims. These half-moon glasses made the world a clearer place, allowing him to work with ease. Unfortunately, today was a harsh day to be working, regardless of clarity.

The last day of the week was always the slowest. Three customers in thrice as many hours. Closing time came as he locked the doors, ready to lock down his own mind for the night.

The store was older than he, and it showed. Every corner housed a family of bugs, each thick window pane was chipped and misty, and more troubling was the wooden beams holding it all together. Each one was plum rotten, ready to cave under the abandoned housing overhead.

Unlike most shopkeepers, Ish preferred the rough eastern streets of Valordolt to the market district's panache. As a result his store had endured several construction projects, finding itself buried beneath a second floor of residence. Being cramped on either side, he and his business had no room to grow anymore.

By Jack Robinson

Maybe this was good for a man of such age. Growth was best left to those with a full set of teeth… the better half of them, at least.

Business wasn't booming, and this meant Ish's little haven was jam-packed with all manner of clocks, parts, odds, ends, and all else betwixt. A few dozen shelves across the walls held tonnes of metal pieces, all forged from brass and quartz, each playing a vital role in a clock's grand scheme.

In the face of a bad day, an old adage came to mind. *Fiat,* Castern for 'let it be done,' was a term coined by judges, clerics, and businessmen the world over. Ish was no different, and he warded off disgruntlement with this single word. Life was so simple with the right motivation.

Waving the weary shop goodnight, he extinguished the candles one by one. The heat was small, unable to warm his flesh. Similarly, his inner flame was dim, and failed to brighten up the dark, spring night. The month of Rainfall was upon Magnus and marked the end of the moon's dominance over her brother: the mighty sun.

Stone Soul

If the tales were to be believed, t͏d Solaris and his sister Luna battled constan͏trol of the sky. Neither held their dominance ͏han a few months. The god's tales never spark͏in Ish's heart; few things did. Honestly, he f͏m long-winded and childish. Such things we͏ant for the ears of men, only those of boys.

Moving into the back room of the s͏had officially entered his home. Small as a͏ith an outhouse attached, his home was swee͏le claustrophobic. Stuffed in the corner w͏d, which acted as a seat, dining area, and workb͏acks of tools and books filled in what little spac͏ned around the room, and the odour of elde͏k filled the air.

Dragging an oversized teapot onto a s͏usted with decades of use – Ish sat down and in͏ in his favourite pastime. As a mechanist of sorts͏nd pleasure in building more than just clocks͏ever time permitted he would build away in his͏sized home, hoping to replicate life itself.

'Arc-Mech' was the name of the resident ͏a of Magnus. They were built by man to serve m͏uch like angels serve. Most were made by the dozen by orcs in est. Meant to fill the ranks of armies or labou factories, their lives were designed witho ng.

But Ish foun in slavery, whether it be man or machine in here others sought to build Arc-Mechs for made them for play.

His last pro china named Sicilla, was finished a yea d left to explore the Casterlands. She was the c ng he had to a daughter. He'd never missed g more. All he wanted was a carrier pigeo rier to drop him a letter. He wanted his c e okay.

Since Sicil arture he'd manage to build a second chil east half of one. With its legs and matrix miss boy still needed some months' more care; ould be worth the wait.

The crea life was once a sacred thing belonging to the god But, with the turn of the Sixth Era, godhood so exclusive anymore. Ish never took such prid work, preferring to be *a* father, not *the* father. Ye rough the night, a smile was stuck to his face. as sacred and his to mould.

Hours of tinkering passed, several cups of tea were drunk, and as the city's grand clock tower struck eleven Ish hit the hay. Of course, being the proprietor of a clock shop, his ears first endured the choir of a hundred different chimes. All eleven rung together: exactly calibrated. He liked his job, loved his life, and wanted it to never change.

But fate had other ideas. The bounds of sleep would have to wait. A heavy hand knocked four times on his door. *Boom bom boom bom*, it rattled, sounding as if a club was beating upon it.

At this hour only fiends walked the streets; the Order never patrolled the east side anymore. If Valordolt's youth were looking for a quick source of bronze roth coins, Ish wasn't going to indulge their greed.

From under the crooked bed he drew a flintlock pistol: old and faithful, it had saved him from thieves more than once. Just last month back a flashy man and his brooding sister had tried their luck, only to meet the barrel of his rustic firearm.

He slowly moved back into the store, toward the door. Each step was quicker than the last as he loaded a lead pellet into the lone chamber of the pistol. In a brave voice, barely showing his trembling tone, he bellowed to the knocker.

"If you're one of Don's boys, jog on; I've no patience for ya. I'm armed and know my rights," he warned.

No answer came from behind the door, panicked or otherwise. So with a fast pull, Ish yanked open the oak barrier and pointed old faithful at the guest.

Standing on his dilapidated porch was an overwhelming figure that stood at almost twice his height and so broad you could confuse him for one of the city's walls. Covered from head to toe in a brown cloak, the identity of this 'man' was an anxious mystery.

Calling this thing a man was a guess at best. Its breaths were monotone and false and its shape was too big for any human on Magnus. Ish even felt a glowing heat from standing in its presence. Sticking out from the shadowed cloak were two unmoving eyes, having a yellow hue and shaped like diamonds. The eyes weren't unnerving, which was the scary part; this thing was inherently friendly.

"I suggest you lower that arm. I mean you no harm," spoke the creature, in a bland voice.

"And I suggest you walk away, chap. I don't want what you're selling."

"I'm not selling anything. I only carry news. News about Sicilla." This last sentence was given with a pinch of regret and instantly sparked worry in Ish's belly. "May I come in?" pled the figure.

The being had him at 'Sicilla'. As if fate itself had willed it, there stood the answer to the last of Ish's problems. Without retracting his weapon, the elder stood aside with a slight nod of acceptance.

"Yes. Yes you may. Just keep your distance, stranger," Ish warned.

Clearing space out back was an impossibility, so the two took seats by the store's counter; Ish in his usual place, while the figure took the seat of a customer. Neglecting to remove his hood, the towering oddity further refused to reveal itself.

"Best I keep this on. My face isn't one you'll want to remember. You can call me Zarpadon, if you please. It may make things easier."

"*Easier?* What do you mean, Zarpadon?" Taking a moment to breathe, Ish readied for the worse. But a clear idea of what was to come lingered in his mind; an undesired, but likely scenario.

"Mr. Peacock." Zarpadon paused and was unsure whether to resume. Eventually, after a moment, the figure could stomach the ticking clocks no longer and continued. "I'm afraid Sicilla is no longer with us," he sighed.

Ish never had 'real' children, but truly believed this is what it was like to lose one. A harrowing emptiness overcame him, no words came to mind or left his mouth; only a burning ache flooded in. Heartache, headache, his very soul ached from the news. Tears lingered on his eyelids and lumps appeared in his throat. His little girl was gone.

"I..." he whimpered.

"No, please, do not speak. Save the words for later, sir. Just remain calm," reasoned Zarpadon.

"Tell me what happened." Ish replied with anger, an emotion he'd believed was lost to him. "Tell me what happened to my Sicilla!"

Zarpadon was still and only lowered his head like a shamed pup. The cloaked figure admitted something no sane being ever would. "It was me. I caused her end."

"What?" Ish said in a cold rage.

"It was my hand that... killed Sicilla."

Never in Ish's long life had the idea of murder ever surfaced. Even now, all he wanted was Zarpadon's suffering, not his life. Yet, a force beyond him seemed to take control. With a swift motion, up came his pistol as it blasted lead onto the self-admitted murderer.

The force was strong on both ends, snapping Ish's own elbow out of place while launching Zarpadon back into a row of grandfather clocks. The noise of the bullet rung in his ears, followed by the cries of a dozen clocks smashing. In one moment, Ish went from humble olden to hapless killer. At least, that was what he thought. Soon to be proven wrong, the cloaked mystery arose from the gunshot, seemingly unharmed.

"I don't understand," Ish gawked.

The cloaked thing stood upright to reveal his wounds. The bullet *had* hit, but neither flesh nor bone: rather a thick wall of pink crystal. No blood poured, and only a few glowing glass fragments fell to the floor; each chimed like a bell as they landed.

"There's plenty you don't understand," added Zarpadon, huffing his words. "I was told you'd be angry, not bloodthirsty. Still, I did deserve that. Truth be told, I spent so long shut away that I forgot what pain feels like."

"You're… an angel?" Crystal bodies belonged to the angels of Prime. If Zarpadon bled pink not red, then an angelic crystivine lingered beneath that cloak.

"Of a sort. I haven't gone by that descriptor for a long time," Zarpadon admitted.

"So you *are* an angel. Your kind are supposed to protect life, not end it. Why did you kill my girl!?"

Still limply waving his emptied pistol about, Ish felt anger building again. One shot wasn't enough to settle his grief. Would any amount suffice?

"Please, lower that thing. Allow me to explain. I was being metaphorical, *mostly*." After retaking his solemn stance, the angel explained the best he could. "My *actions* got her killed, my failures. Sicilla sacrificed herself to save me. She took her own life, but only to save mine."

This angel had a poor way with words. If what he said rang true, then she was still gone, but it wasn't in vain. Helping Zarpadon back to his chair, they continued to talk of her passing.

"Why did she give herself up? Cilla had a happy life. What could warrant such a thing?" Ish asked in confusion.

"Her, myself, and my company of paladins venture into a dark place. This place was corrupted to the core and would've been all our ends, if not for Sicilla." Through his bland voice you could almost make out a sense of pride in Zarpadon's words. "She ended her life a hero."

"Paladins? You're part of the Order!" snapped Ish. "Explains a lot."

Ish never trusted the boys in black. The religious movement practically built this city, but that was a long time ago. Now, the sect had never been weaker. With a dying fool as its leader and a council of ignorant youths in place to contradict him, the Order brought very little actual order to the realm.

"Not anymore," assured Zarpadon, "You see, my boss is breaking away from the paladins. He holds goals far grander."

By Jack Robinson

"He's a smart man. But what's grander than our 'mighty' Order."

"The very world is at stake. If we don't act, Magnus and Prime *will* die."

"*Okay.* That's pretty big." Ish was unsure if Zarpadon was preaching heresy, or he was the only true devotee left in Valordolt. But, seeing as Sicilla had supposedly trusted the angel, so would he. For a time.

"Oh, the biggest. Truth is, time is short, and I need your help."

"What could a divine being need me for?"

Waving coyly, Ish groaned at his recently-popped elbow. The pain was a chronic numbness; the worst kind of pain, ever-present and pervasive.

"Here, allow me…" Zarpadon held great speed for a being so broad. With a flash of pink in his hand, the angel snapped the elbow back into place with a single movement, one devoid of pain. "As I said: time is short. I need you to make me something. It's in your field of expertise, I'm sure of it. I need… a special clock."

A 'special clock' was a vague request. Vague and pointless to boot. Zarpadon was mocking him, surely.

"I need more than that. What makes it so special? Is it of the 'cuckoo' variety? A ball-bearing model?"

"I'm afraid not. It doesn't tell time at all. Rather it bends it."

Zarpadon was definitely mocking him. Time was untouchable, even by the Great Lord Gideon or any of the lesser gods up on Prime. Like with the pistol, a raging void of loss came over Ish. One less deserved, but present, all the same.

"You'd come to me, break my very heart and soul, *then* ask of something so queer? Please *leave*. Let me grieve for my girl," Ish snapped.

"I'm not being queer. I need you, Ish. I beg–"

Granting a second chance, Ish harshly said, "Then be honest. What is it you *really* need?"

"I need a custom clock, one built to my leader's specifications. It *can* truly bend time. This is all we've got to go on here. Please, grant me a single ounce of trust."

Again, breaking a man down, only to ask for an object an old mechanist could never muster, wasn't polite; it wasn't even funny. It was time for the angel to leave. The day was drawing to a close and the old man was tired. Tired of the day and of life.

"Then I suggest you go to uptown and talk with the Engineer's Guild. I've got to make arrangements for Sicilla's burial." Ish pointed Zarpadon to the door and hushed any further debate. "Good day, sir!"

Without a fuss, the angel nodded and left him to his sadness. Sicilla had moved on and they both needed to as well.

<u>Chapter 2: A Part To Play</u>

Philip was a man on a mission. When his boss gave an order, he was quick to action. Especially when a plan like theirs was so close to fruition. Months of bootlicking and playing politics had been a gripping and exhausting ride for the young man, and now it was about to come to a head.

Tonight was the night he'd been training for. Since joining the Order he'd been given a modest station at Hericore's side, learning to spot the tricks and how to avoid all the faux pas. Now it was time to put this knowledge to use.

Philip's official title in the Order was 'High Steward': he was a man meant to tend to the whims of the religion's upper echelon. Hericore, however, had shackled Philip to a far less gracious position during day-to-day discourse. Philip was what you'd colloquially call a 'courier.' He was a man who ferried notes from paladin to paladin, from Hericore to the rest of Valordolt.

Being a glorified mailman wasn't appealing to Philip. Frankly he hated every minute. But he also knew it was the best way to learn from the best the land had to offer. He'd eavesdrop on the words of a dozen others, able to pick apart each point they had to make and retort to it in complete silence once he'd left their presence.

In time he'd grown a hefty opinion of his wordsmithing skills. He could forge an illethium blade from nothing but pig-iron when it came to social smithery. A skill he was finally allowed to put into practice.

Philip combed back his tides of wavy curls, robed himself in the darkest of suits, and carefully picked a fitting masquerade mask for the occasion. He was going to the opera.

The right task often required the right mask, and Philip had crafted just the one for tonight. The man he was destined to meet was the sternest fellow the Order had to offer. Colder than the tip of a northerner's nose, this man rarely left the confines of his social circle and everyone preferred it that way. He warded the city's prison with an equally chilling shoulder.

The Warden was a figure of little care, but infinite patience. Like a pouncing beast, he had one goal in life and wouldn't rest until it was over. Such a man seemed impossible to breach, an unreachable personality beneath an impenetrable exterior. Luckily, this was Philip's job: to deliver to people and places others wouldn't dare approach. After all, what was a courier if not persistent?

They would meet atop the tallest viewing box at Valordolt's largest opera house. Resting over two storeys above the common rabble, the box was meant for snobs of a certain breed. The kind of snob that hated the company of fellow snobs.

The opera house itself was situated in the comfort of Valordolt's northern sector, a place where its upper-classmen resided. Perfectly designed in its construction, the house was measured with acoustics in mind. Every word spoke on stage would travel just as far as it needed to, reaching each member of the audience with precisely the right impact.

As Philip crept up to the viewing boxes, he was hit with the perfect voices as they rolled up the arched walls and through the fluted viewing box like wind passing across a still everglade. Philip only hoped to achieve this level of perfection one day, and the opera below only served as further inspiration.

By Jack Robinson

'*Every singer and stagehand has a part to play, from the leading lady to the lowly flute player. It is an unspoken truth: both, regardless of glory, make the performance work. If the flute player stops for even a second, then everything will be off beat, and chaos will soon follow. Such a lowly role contains just as much power as the lead,*' Philip philosophised.

"Thoughts should remain in your head," said the Warden with a soft and grumpy tone. His voice was like a sigh stretched across an entire sentence. "Plus, speaking aloud can betray one's image."

Philip froze in place like a snubbed pup, only now realising what he'd just done. Or rather what he just said. Every word he'd just thought had leaked out of his big mouth. He slapped his forehead with disappointment and issued a false apology to the Warden.

"I apologise. Not for my words, but for my decorum," Philip said with a bow. "Can I start over?"

He didn't know why he said the things he said out loud, he just did. Philip had an unnatural talent for doing that which he felt 'right,' even when it didn't always seem so. He'd called this talent 'shining silver luck,' long ago, but at this point it didn't seem like plain old luck.

"You may not," denied the Warden. The man didn't move away from the opera, his eyes fixated on the perfection below. "First impressions are everything, and you blew yours. Perhaps your message will redeem your recklessness?"

"Very well. I'm an envoy of our Arch-Paladin. He has sent me to discuss our little business arrangement," Philip said. "He said that–"

"Hold on," interrupted the Warden. "'Our?' I think you mean to say 'your,' kid. 'Core and I had the agreement, not us. I don't know who in the hells you are."

It was meant as a slight on Philip's reputation, and it stung as intended. But, sensing the price of retaliation, Philip bit his lip and corrected himself once more.

"Of course. I am but a lowly hazelnut shrub in a garden of majestic walnut trees," said Philip.

His turn of phrase was enough to turn the Warden's head from the show in a moment of perplexed awe.

"That's a mighty specific analogy. You work with a lotta nuts, kid? Is Hericore a bit nutty these days, aye?"asked the Warden with a sly smile. "Sit. We'll talk more during the intermission. I wish to enjoy one more hour of heaven before enduring another night of bureaucratic hell."

Doing as instructed, Philip perched himself on the back of the seat beside the Warden. He stood out in such a bohemian pose, but he did enjoy sitting above his peers. It was a small victory, and Philip lived for any win regardless of its size.

They stared down at the final throes of the tiring singers. These grand acts lasted so long that most productions rotated an entire second cast in to play for the latter acts. A bold but wise strategy for any group. Philip often wondered who would replace his allies once their roles finally burnt out.

To see the leading lady all pampered and pristine felt almost insulting to Philip. The girl was no older than he, barely a woman by the laws of the Order. Yet she found herself in a pompous grey wig that drooped past her breasts, and wearing a monobrow clearly painted on her face with a generous application. Its fakery was sickening.

Stone Soul

The rich occupants of the theatre hall wanted the voice of an angel but the looks of a haggish spinster. It wasn't the wisdom they sought in age, it was the illusion of its existence. It mattered not if the girl was wise, she only needed to seem it. This kept a lingering disgust in Philip's throat till the long-awaited intermission arrived.

As soon as the curtain dropped, the Warden was snapped back to reality. He failed to engage with Philip at first, and remained silent as he disappeared to the privy. Minutes later he returned with a bottle in his hand, along with two glasses.

"Welcome to hell, Philip," the Warden said. "This is my own personal Tarus. I'm stuck in an eternal loop of pleasing the Order like a shaved monkey. If you seek to follow in your master's footsteps, I'd honestly reconsider."

The scowl on the Warden's face was replaced with a hollow look of happiness in his words. He poured himself a glass of the eastern port before offering Philip a tipple too. An offer that was impossible to refuse, but also difficult to enforce. Philip did not need to drink the sweet wine, only accept its presence.

"Thank you, Warden. It is nice to see some true gentlemen in our ranks," Philip said.

"Yes, the Order does tend to put the 'lad' in paladin. All too chummy, if you ask me. Now, this business?" The Warden sipped his wine and continued hastily. "The old coot wanted to see my mad dog. Why, after two decades, he has taken an interest in the loon is beyond me, but I don't just share my secrets with anyone. Not even the mighty 'lord of the land.'"

The 'old coot' he was referring to was Hericore. After his months of service, Philip was always learning new insults for the withered leader, and 'old coot' managed to hit his mind in just the right way.

"You've heard the rumours, I'm sure? The ones of the 'old coot's' condition? Well, it's not the whole truth, not at all. He's not dying… yet. But he's looking for allies for the day he does pass. People like you, Warden.'"

Philip pretended to sip a small sample of wine, imitating the Warden's own actions with greater acting than the painted trollops below. He knew the make of wine well, an old eastern batch from the Casterlands, Philip's home. He'd grown up with grape merchants and never hated anything more than the stagnant taste of fermented swill. It would betray his very core to swallow even a drop of the expensive port.

Philip continued, unclouded by the lazy haze of alcohol. "When he does leave this world, he needs to make sure certain goals are met. A man, even one like him, needs to die with peace of mind. So he says, anyway."

"He visited the mad dog to vet me? To check me out like some old busted mustang?" the Warden deduced.

"Technically, yes. I like to see it as more of a test. One seeking moral fibre," Philip smirked.

Hart gave an understanding raise of the eyebrow before he corrected, "Or lack thereof?"

Sharp as a kiwi from the southern shores, the Warden understood Hericore's tactics ten paces in advance. If Philip wanted to achieve a victory tonight, he'd need to adopt a new strategy. The Warden was a sour soul, and sweetness was only going to sit poorly on his tongue. This theory was backed by the port that neither of them had actually swallowed thus far.

If sweet or sour wouldn't reach the Warden, then bitterness maybe the only alternative.

"He's not like that. Hericore is a good person," Philip said. His words didn't stretch far from the truth, but just far enough. "One of the best in the Order. He has big plans. Ones even death can't interfere with."

At the mere mention of the word 'good,' the Warden's jaw tightened and his expression became consumed by a deeper self.

"There it is. The first words I've believed true all night," the Warden said as he gestured up at the shining gemstones encrusted into the roof of the opera house. "Gods, I hate you visionary sorts. Y- You spend so much time staring up at the 'big picture' that you fail to notice the harsh reality right before you." The man continued to rant and rave, pointing to the diamonds above and the wooden stage below. Not a single word offended Philip this time. He'd achieved the first act of his plan. "The air of a visionary is a stinking one. The smell of your own ass gas overpowers the roses – makes it impossible for you to smell them."

"I'm not like that," Philip denied. "Hericore is. That we can agree one. But not me."

As for the second deceptive act, Philip pulled a piece of scarlet paper from his inner breast pocket. It was an ornately styled message printed on a folded work of art; origami in the shape of a rose.

"A letter," Philip explained. "A proposal. An alliance. Perhaps a more agreeable solution than Hericore's."

Whether or not the note was from the Arch-Paladin was now irrelevant. He'd stoked a burning scorn within the Warden. An angered man thought a little less, and all Philip had to do was place the illusion of the note's owner. The Warden held the note and began to bear a cooler head, but only for a moment.

"You're rather sneaky for a mailman," said the Warden.

"Hey, delivering letters is my job. Nothing more," Philip replied coyly.

"This is *your* agreement then?" asked the Warden.

"That's the one," lied Philip.

The busy Warden wasted no time in unfolding the artistry and pondering the contents of the letter. His eyes maniacally glossed the red paper and came to a snappy conclusion.

"You're an interesting fellow, Philip. You want one of your boys working in my prison? Rather illegal to forgo the hiring methods of the Order, don't you think?" the Warden questioned.

Philip took another fake sip of wine and replied, "This man wouldn't find work the 'normal' way. He's nuttier than the old coot is. Another reason why we wanted to see your dog: to see how you'd fare with a similar case of the crazies. I want him dead, but Hericore wants him… around for further uses."

"Uses that'll be clearer once 'Core's in the ground?" the Warden asked.

Again, Philip had to tell a half truth. The boy's name was Krell, and a boy he was not. The aged hunk of madness and meat was nothing more than a mentally gimped pawn of Hericore. A pawn easily slipped under the Warden's nose for their grand scheme. Not that Philip would allow this information to carelessly slip out like his thoughts before.

"Exactly," confirmed Philip. "There's more to this 'boy' than meets the eye. If we keep him under our eye, then he can't escape once Hericore gives. That's *my* offer."

As things below them began to return, lanterns igniting and audience seating, the Warden found himself running out of time to dig deeper into the offer. If he was a calmer man, the Warden may have even taken the time to see through the ruse. Fortunately, he was not.

"Alright, listen, kid. Listen, because I'm not in the right mood to repeat myself," began the Warden. "That nut is as good as a golden goose under my wing, assuming you can track down a goose of my own. Last week some slimy loanshark by the name of Donsis was meant to stand trial before the High Council for his crimes, one of which being an arrogant prick. Arrogance did what arrogance does and he bounced, leaving me and the whole council – including righteous Hericore – coughing on his dust."

Hericore did mention this little event to Philip. Donsis was an elven inmate held behind bars for months on a technicality, only to mysteriously post bail days before trial. What the rat waited that long for was unimportant. What *did* matter was his decision to run.

It was a 'happy coincidence' that the arrogant ass in question was the same thing the Arch-Paladin and his coy courier were seeking. Funny how the Warden, despite all his cunning, ended up the same place Philip had intended from the start.

"So," the Warden continued to prattle. "I want you to track down this elvish rat for me, and save me another night of hell. A favour to only strengthen our budding alliance. One of my captains spotted him hiding out around Andover Avenue along the 'Miracle Mile'. I want him back at court and in one piece, if you're feeling fancy. Get it done and done right."

With a smirk of gratitude, Philip obliged. "Of course, Warden."

As the show fired up once more, the courier took his leave. The Warden waved him away after placing the port bottle firmly into his grip. It was meant as a show of good faith, but Philip sought to toss the bitter liquid along with his bitter act the second he was out of sight.

"Feel free to finish the show, kid," called Hart, who returned to focusing on the opera. "The rat can wallow in his hole a while longer."

With another pair of acts left to endure Philip had to decline. One round of fakery was bad enough, and he doubted he could last another, let alone a third. His declination was barely audible over the rising song of a sick stage, likened to Magnus' own ill state.

Once enveloped in shadow and far from the Warden's view, he stopped and slipped off his masks. The cooling blackness of night was upon him and felt better than any fancy attire he pretended to enjoy.

As for the wine, he'd no need for such a poison. It was the duty of lesser men to drink the stuff. Since a lesser man could not be found, a lesser woman would do. Just out of the opera house's view wallowed a weary soul camped out in the mud of a nearby embankment.

She was a young street urchin and held the bluest eyes one could ever want to gaze into. But Philip had no love for blue eyes or the kind of attraction usually attached to them. Especially a streetwalking loner like her.

Women were more than a nice pair of eyes to him, they were an asset, and this girl was no use to anyone anymore. No one that slept in the dirt could be useful.

Handing the bottle of opened port to her, Philip pulled an awkward smile. He was quick to leave, freeing himself of her foul presence and empty thanks.

He was only interested in the weighty praise of those that mattered.

"'Thank yee mistur," slurred the woman. It was unfortunate her slur was caused by more than simply debauchery. She'd clearly got something loose in her noggin' and it roused an unwanted twinge of sorrow in Philip's heart. "I'll be forever inya debt."

With the Warden dealt with and the faux bargain made, it was time for phase two of the plan. Removing a second red letter from his pocket Philip gazed upon it. The word 'Donsis' was marked across it in the same shining font as Hart's.

"One more message to deliver, boss," Philip smirked before heading off into the darkness ahead.

Chapter 3: Black Blood

Kalsec saw red in all that he did. Anger in his vision, blood in the violence the anger led to, and after all was said and done, he'd smell rusty ferrous in the air once again as the cycle repeated day after day. This had been his life since his birth and things were unlikely to change.

Tonight he needed a cool head, or a lukewarm one at least. He had caught the eager eye of an evil man. A man who sought what he held close: a weapon of great power.

As the young Kalsec strolled from the city, this weapon glimmered in the light of the great milky moon above. The sign of the night could be seen across all of Magnus, and tonight's half moon would bode well for the pale boy. A half moon was the symbol of potential and divided people with its meaning; some said it was optimistically full, some said it was pessimistically empty.

Kalsec was man of pure optimism. Nothing was gained from doubting one's path. If someone wanted his blade then they sought to muddy his path, and this could not happen.

After a quick jaunt from Valordolt proper, the small hamlet of Igial Lane came into view. A pitiful holding full of degenerates, but the perfect place to wine and dine with the fine swine of the divine in decline. If he was to meet with this evil man, he'd choose no other place.

Sitting within smelling-distance of Valordolt's sewage system, Igial's Lane held a murky density in the air. A pungent sensation of warm rubbish burned at the nose and was enough to make even Kalsec's cold face flinch. It was no surprise the people of this hamlet were so vile. Spend enough time living with filth and you start to imitate it, become it. This was a feeling Kalsec had every day on this stinking world.

By the old chapel stood a rotting inn by the name of 'Trawler's', a place that disparate sailors of west coast once came to drown their sorrows over their drowned cabin mates. It was inside Trawler's Inn that Kalsec would gain a chance to sit in the presence of the haggling hieratic and absorb what wisdom they had to offer.

Outside of the inn sat a dwarf and his posse of prats, each more inebriated than the last. Sickly men, lumpy dwarfs, and a lone tattooed centaur made up this group of fools. They'd enough strength amongst them to kill a few dozen men, yet they daren't even attempt to glare a lingering look Kalsec's way. They were drunken fools, but even they knew better than to challenge a blade as fine as his.

Inside the ugly inn were uglier patrons and the ugliest barmaid on all of Magnus. They were silent to his presence and left him to his business, their sole redeeming quality.

At the back of the room of rotted wood and hanging herbs was a shadowy booth reserved for the boy. The booth was already occupied by the masked eccentric that had sought him out.

"Evening, Syphus." Kalsec spoke in calm and authoritative tone. He'd perfected the art of commanding others with a certain tone of voice. A cold call that cut through any semblance of weakness. It even managed to overshadow the nasally knot at the back of his throat. "I hope you found this place well?"

By Jack Robinson

The collector of dark treasures and even darker
secrets, Syphus wasn't a stranger to him, but by no
means a friend. Up in the north, a kingdom of elegant
elves lived amongst nature. It was a land built on the
back of a recent dynasty, one aided into power by
Syphus. After helping win over an entire nation, the
mysterious masked man had little to do other than to
absorb the knowledge of the world around him.
Eventually, this led him to hunting down all manner of
artefacts, which now brought him to Kalsec's booth.

"Finding the place wasn't hard, lad. It was finding
the courage to stay and weather the stench," said
Syphus with a sour face.

"Comfort isn't a luxury I can afford. Even as a man of
class I must often sacrifice things for the mission of my
life." Kalsec ordered some black wine to the table, a
drink both men enjoyed. Wasting no further time, the
pale boy placed a hand on his blade and said, "Shall we
dive straight into the proceedings?"

The look he received back was one of
disappointment. Syphus shook his head as a faint grin
peeked from the wiry gap in his mask. A familiar piece
of face wear that Kalsec had once worn, the mask was a

bitter reminder of a bitter winter he'd spent with a clan of bitter company. It was nice to see Syphus had the wealth to buy his way into such a memory.

"My, you have been alone too long," Syphus said. "I, along with most civilised folk, don't just skip the interesting parts. If I'm to buy that blade of yours, I *need* its history. The tale is half the value when it comes to such a fine piece."

"It is no extraordinary tale. Quite the sordid affair," Kalsec claimed.

"Obviously. I'm sure I've heard it before. But that doesn't devalue its existence, merely adds to the enjoyment." Syphus poured another glass and beckoned the past from Kalsec's lips. "Tell away, lad."

"Very well," Kalsec began. "It all started five years back…"

***

The air around Valordolt was chilly past midnight. A black sky darkened the streets of Old Valour, the original town that grew into the city of Valordolt, like a cancer on the countryside. A waning moon above shone a slender spectre of white light across the city's soft blue lake, shining sombrely in the night.

One of the few things Kalsec could smile at was the calming feel of water in his ears and on his skin. There was something hypnotic about a good and gentle wave upon the body. It was as if his soul was being cleansed of any scorn that gripped it. If only salvation was that easy to come by.

His anger wasn't all bad, anyhow. It was pure passion, expressed in the only way he knew how. There was a gap at his core, one that could only be filled by taking what wasn't his. Sometimes this would be physical, other times he was content with leeching the joy from another's expression. A parasite on society, he was. But that didn't make him any less of a person. Most cowered from being hated, but Kalsec only relished in it.

The only sack of meat on Magnus that didn't seem to despise him wholly was an equally despicable wretch by the name of Alva. They'd met years back, when he was the student and she, the teacher. Over time their roles flipped. Now she considered herself an apprentice to the boy's ego.

Some were more susceptible to charm than others. She was near impervious to it. Alva had a permanent scowl on her gaunt face, one earned from a lifetime of disappointment. Whatever Kalsec had done to win her favour must've been a good one. Even he questioned her unwavering loyalty to him and nothing set him on edge more than not knowing.

Perhaps she knew this, and that was the secret pleasure she longed for. Pleasure purchased with uneasy confusion. Regardless, the two had rarely been apart since school, a boy and his senior, now a man and his admirer. With a little luck and a lot of ambition they'd soon be a god and his apostle.

While the rugged Kalsec strolled along the lakeside in a patchwork longcoat, the more refined Alva gracefully stepped behind in a lacy dress adorned with onyx jewels. Her goal was simple: to draw attention. His was a little more covert, to never be noticed.

Alva was no looker. With a twig-like form – all slender and crooked – she was never meant for romancing. It was her implied wealth that was meant to draw the eyes of onlookers. Nothing was more attractive to humans than a rich whore, and she acted the part well.

After a half hour of traipsing about the lake's many piers, a duo of delinquents showed themselves. Both swaggered by the incognito Kalsec without batting an eyelid. One was thin, one was fat, and both stunk of sickly sweet port and something sour beneath it. They saw him as nothing but a bum, a non-issue, and perhaps the least attractive thing a human eye could see. That was the plan.

The pair of overall-wearing workers stopped before Alva, looking her over from the tiara in her hair to the rings on her fingers. It didn't take long for them to buzz closer into the lacy trap.

"Well 'ello there, ma'am," said the fat man with a dishonest removal of his cap. "Can't 'elp but notice you're without an escort this fine night."

"We're always willin' to keep a dame safe. Ain't we, cuz?" followed the thin man.

Dishonourable fools, the pair of them. They were seeking to thieve the gems the second her guard was down. Little did they know there was no honour

between the predators and prey, and Alva's guard
never faltered.

"We sure are," the fat man grinned. "Whaddaya say,
ma'am? Could be fun, ya know?"

The fat man extended his arm to Alva whilst the thin
man crept his own behind his back, reaching for a
rusted blade. It had come, the moment Kalsec had
waited for all night. It was time for the crimson cloud to
return and he savoured every second.

"Well, gentlemen," Alva softly said. Flattered, she
placed a hand on her chest and let out a small gasp.
"I'm not one to refuse a *fun time*."

Kalsec snuck behind the duo of dockmen with a
blade of his own readied. It was a small shoto he'd
picked off the corpse of an eastern warrior. Small but
effective, just how he liked his weapons. No one could
counter an attack they couldn't see coming.

Alva's hand moved closer to her chest as she drew an
ebony wand from her bosom. It was near invisible in
the dark of the night and the fat man had no clue of
what torturous fate awaited him. A magic far worse
than the arcane arts, cast from a witch as black as the
spells she mastered.

By Jack Robinson

A muted flash of black energy shot from the wand's tip, cocooned in a yolk of wispy white. It was a jolt of the dark arts, a combination of the arcane, the ephemeral, and the necrotic disciplines. It was life, death, and undeath hitting a man at once, a seemingly endless feeling of death and rebirth as the fat man's body flew back like a feather on a breeze.

Whatever was left of the fat man writhed and twitched on the wooden pier, usually a short existence followed a direct blast of dark magic. Human bodies were tough, but they always gave in to the endless cycle of pain Alva propagated. Now all that was left was the thin man.

Though shocked at his cousin's state, the thin man refused to let the attack halt his own. Unflinching in the face of pain, the man aimed his knife right between Alva's emotionless eyes. She'd a gaze empty of joy or focus, even amidst such a calamity. She feared not, as they'd done this dance a hundred times all across the land.

The thin man's stab stopped an inch from her face. He was frozen in place as a crooked shoto became wedged between his shoulder blades. It took a good yank, but Kalsec pulled the thin man away from his underling with a smile on his face.

His shoto reached a stop in the thin man's heart as Kalsec reached the climax of the moment. The softer feeling of the organs always made for a wash of relief in Kalsec's own heart. Once the heart had stopped, then the battle was won.

"Don't take this too hard, my friend. No sense in dragging any shame to the afterlife with you," Kalsec whispered in the thin man's ear. "You're only human, after all."

As the thin man started to go limp, a strange smell filled the air as viscous fluids leaked from the shoto's wound. Blood always looked black in the moonlight, if the smelly liquid was indeed blood.

"I swear they stink worse and worse," frowned Alva.

"Yes," groaned Kalsec with an odd look on his face.

"A bit late to grow a conscience?" she said, noting the look.

"It's not that. They just seemed a little different, is all." Kalsec rubbed the dark fluid that'd spilt onto his gloves. "Their blood's thicker than usual."

By Jack Robinson

To Kalsec, gloves were a ward against the dirt of the world. A ward now endangered by this vile corruption that stuck to them. It needed to end. His hands needed to be cleansed of any and all filth.

Alva frowned again and shrugged, "Must've been diseased or some such. Wouldn't be the first. Best case 'em and move on before the Order shows up."

Whilst fumbling in the thin man's dungarees, Kalsec found an assortment of jewellery buried in the depths of his pockets. The shining rings and necklaces all held small gems at their cores and each was a different shape and size. Knowing his victims were genuine monsters and crooks made gutting them all the sweeter.

"Alva, there must be at least a few thousand roths worth of gems here," Kalsec grinned as one of the topaz stones reflected the moonlight. In the gem's vague reflection was a glint of danger as he spied Alva being grappled behind him. "Alva?!"

Kalsec turned back to see the mangled body of the fat man attempting to tear Alva in two. Even with half his head corroded by dark magic, the fat freak fought with the tenacity of a wild florankhi. This feat of impossible endurance was enough to hold Kalsec's eye for just a second, a second that would prove to be his undoing.

A chilling pain shot through Kalsec like a bolt of lightning as a sharp row of teeth became buried in his shoulder. It was the thin man, alive and well, digging his jaw into the rogue. 'Alive,' wasn't the best term to describe these monsters. If they still fought without head nor heart they were nothing but soulless husks now. Given their pungent aroma, maybe they always were?

"You gents are full of surprises," groaned Alva beneath two hundred pounds of undead flesh. She pulled a lengthy lace from her corset and began to spin it like a lasso. "Hows about I give you one back?"

"Stop showboating and blast these curs!" Kalsec demanded, dancing around the dock in an attempt to shake off the thin pest. The pleasure he'd usually derive from pain fed only Alva as she whipped her lace around the fat man's chunky neck.

Calling on one more wave of magic, she managed to cut clean through the man's throat as if her lace was sharper than illethium wire. Even an undead couldn't exist without a head.

By Jack Robinson

Before he knew it, Kalsec was also freed from the thin man's grasp as Alva whipped him away with the lace. Leaving nothing to chance anymore, Kalsec finished things by placing his shoto deep in the man's eye socket.

"Rare to see the guppy bite back," Kalsec said as he savoured the gouging. Each twist of the shoto was made with malice, vengeance for his pulsing shoulder. "I'd like to watch you snap back now."

Tempting fate was the act of a fool. All of existence was a fine balance of bound and rebound. To think fate wasn't real was to deny the sun and moon also. Those were things Kalsec knew to be real with gods to back them. Yet, he still refused the consequences of his actions, acting as if fate was no more than a lie made to inspire hopelessness in the world.

As the thin man's hands both reached up to claw at Kalsec's face, he'd never regretted a statement more.

"You should learn to keep that trap of yours shut," Alva said as she watched the fat man rise headless and lame.

Undead were never this tough in the past. These ghouls were something more, something beyond the beyond.

"Unlikely," Kalsec replied.

As much as their lives were in danger, the pair had never had so much fun.

After some more struggling, Kalsec soon lost his blade in the thin man's skull. Such a fine weapon falling to such a pointless foe was a sign that the pair were outmatched, much to their denial. A fact Kalsec had to accept to survive.

Taking Alva's hand in his, Kalsec gave a simple order, "Hoff it."

With the sound of growling and groaning behind them, both Kalsec and his ward made for safety, wherever that was. Valordolt wasn't a friendly place, especially for two folks of a fiendish nature. The Order's light wouldn't shine on them this night.

"Next time you invite me along to one of these little night walks, I must remember to decline," Alva panted.

"All in service to the plan, dear Alva. All in service," reassured Kalsec as he searched the dockside for a safe haven. "Everything is part of the gods' plan. Believe in me. Ah, over there."

Kalsec pointed to a well-lit manor a few hundred yards away. The walled wonder sat taller than all those around it and shone like the topaz in his palm. Its grounds of sculpted hedges and apple trees peeked out over its tall barrier of bricks. Salvation if only for a few moments.

Behind them came the crashing sounds of the fat man as his thin cousin rode atop him like a ghoulish jockey. They hollered the name of a false god as they charged after their prey. Idiots, the pair of them. Aldrich was a god no more, the first and last of the fallen lords of Prime.

"That place'll do," Alva said. "We'll need a distraction whilst we climb. Unless you're willing to offer up a second course to that toothy twerp."

"Just blast the bricks and be done with it," Kalsec suggested, to which he earned a harsh glare.

"Despite your past, you're still just a boy beneath it all, aren't you?" sighed Alva. "'Lest you want them to keep chasing us then the wall stays."

Stone Soul

The sun liked to set, the tides liked to change, and bitches liked to bitch. Alva sought to dig her claws into him at any possible point. Just one more inch of power in their dynamic. But for every inch she took, Kalsec demanded a foot in return. Or in this case, he'd offer his own.

"Fine, but I'll need a little leg up if we're jumping that hurdle," Kalsec bargained.

With a begrudging nod, Alva send a dark sprite of magic spinning at the feet of the ghoulish cousins. It didn't end their hunt, but did delay it just long enough.

As the pair pulled themselves over the walls of salvation, it seemed the escape was in vain. They landed with a crunch as a loud thud soon followed. The ghouls wasted no time bashing themselves into the brickwork, managing to jostle a few loose pieces free. It wouldn't be long until this manor became Kalsec's tomb.

With the heat rising in his shoulder, the boy wasted no time in charging to the manor's back door. If he was to die, he'd at least want a good chair to crumple into. That's if he *was* destined to die, *if* he believed in destiny.

By Jack Robinson

"Get ready for another blast," Kalsec ordered, pointing to the door.

"I don't think so," Alva declined as she showed off her snapped twig of a wand. "No wand, no wonder. You know that."

As they reached the door, things began to seem bleaker than before, somehow. With the ghouls now halfway done with their demolition, defeat slowly crept back into mind. But Kalsec was not easily shied from victory, even once bitten. Upon looking down at his gloves and the black blood drying over them, he was now motivated not just by greed, but also by curiosity. This, and the need to finally rid his gloves of the ooze of putrefaction.

Taking the sharpened remains of his shoto, Kalsec crammed it between the gap in the door. Using the stubby handle he sought to snap open the latch holding their salvation at bay. It was an act of much dexterity and even greater luck.

"I learnt this trick a while back. Before I ever crossed paths with you," boasted Kalsec.

"I expected nothing less from a scoundrel like yourself," Alva said as she ran her bony fingers along his red hot wound. Even when pressed for time she made sure to twist her finger deep into one of the bite holes, making them both quiver: one from pleasure and the other from pain.

"Careful, woman. I enjoy your lack of restraint, most of the time. But now is not it," warned Kalsec, and without complaint Alva withdraw her hand.

As the latch cracked open, the wall soon followed. The ghouls dove to the backdoor just as it closed in their faces. Another brush with defeat earned Kalsec another step closer to victory.

Alva, the healthier of the two, held the door with all her remaining strength. Each bash from the ghouls left her with less and less resolve. Meanwhile, Kalsec's search for a weapon had to be a quick one. To lose now would be simply disappointing.

Kalsec searched the grain shed they found themselves in, and he'd nothing but rusted trowels and frayed ropes to hold off the threat. He needed to delve deeper into the manor.

The adjoining halls of the manor were tight and crooked. Lined with poorly-painted landscapes and dying potted plants, void of light, the manor was more of a damnation than the promised salvation. After another moment of searching and a long venture up what felt like a league of stairs, Kalsec found the first denizen of the decrepit building.

"Evening, soldier," greeted a wrinkled husk of a man. A balding sack of liver spots stood hunched before the boy with a stern face. Wrapped in a linen gown and stinking of an overflowing chamber pot, the elder wasn't all there in the head as he continued, "Fancy meeting a mere squire like you all the way out here, on the frontlines."

Whatever war the elder was referring to was long over. No war had graced Magnus for decades, and Kalsec assumed the elder was thinking of one even older than that. As he tried to sidestep the old man, he kept getting cut off as the two danced in the corridor for what felt like a solid minute.

"Well, whatcha gawking at, new blood. Dig me a new latrine or I'll be setting Captain Kavel on your heiney."

As sickening as it was to see the effects of age on a once mighty man, Kalsec hadn't the time for caring.

Though the old man was likely a proud paladin back in his day, now he was nothing but a waste of skin.

"This isn't the frontline, sir. Just a hole for you and every other veteran of this land to die in," Kalsec informed. "You can retire from the Order, but never from its callous nature."

"Bull," complained the old man. "What's this red stuff on you uniform? Blood? Human blood? Heresy, squire. You're here to kill greenskins and nothin' more. I'm ordering you to head to the captain's tent immediately."

With a heavy sigh, Kalsec snatched the man by the scruff and issued an order of his own.

"Cease your babbling and take a nap, old man. A long, long nap," Kalsec seethed as he tossed the former hero down the staircase with a choir of cracks and snaps. "Dense dimwit."

Looking down the rest of the corridor, it seemed to be much of the same, an endless stretch of rooms, each housing an elderly fellow. Some were fast asleep and others were too buried in their books to notice Kalsec's intrusion. None had what he sought, and Alva's strength waned.

By Jack Robinson

Desperation set in as the giant retirement home became a giant disappointment. All until the corridor came to an end, and a pitch black door waited at it. A door with another latch lock and the silver numbers '*00*' on it. It was dark, it was odd, and it was all Kalsec could think about. It was as if something had drawn him to this very spot on this very night.

"Look out, destiny. Here I come." Kalsec took a deep breath as he entered the menacing room. He'd kill a crook and an old man, but he wasn't ready for what awaited him inside room '*00*.'

<u>Chapter 4: Grave Request</u>

Ish didn't open his store, in the following days since the angel's visit. Hell, he didn't even work on his newest Arc-Mech. The idea of replacing Sicilla seemed bastardising now. Then, before he knew it, the next week had already reached its end.

The last day of the week was always the slowest; nine hours spent in a depressive rut. Never had his bed garnered so much attention. Today was Sicilla's unofficial burial. Zarpadon was vague about her end, and Ish could only assume she resided in an unmarked grave in some god-forsaken field out east.

This wasn't his way of doing it; a kinder end was needed for a kinder breed of girl. Buying a plot in the southern cemetery was all he could afford. This didn't include a gravedigger, meaning the task rested on his own heavy heart.

At sunset, Ish travelled to the yard of the dead. A half-mile from home, his trip was tiring and many odd looks met him along the way. In this week of sadness he'd not shaved or bathed once; common for most, but not for a man of his glossy enamel. Many faces he'd seen every day for years seemed alien. He was always lonely, but never like this.

The grave was against the city's tallest stretch of wall. The sun would never rise on her resting place – caught in the shadow of the Order's might. Like most things in this land.

It wasn't a nice yard either. As he started to dig, a woman, hidden under purple robes, and her roguish centaur guard started picking at the nearby graves. They robbed not just heirlooms, but also bones and other half-rotted parts. They stunk of evil and meat; more so the latter. Ish didn't stop them, but prayed they would never do the same to him once death came knocking.

The robbers seemed interested in 'fresh' produce more than anything. It sickened Ish to think of such a thing. The raw gore of a freshly passed man was not an easy thought to hold. It was one such reason he preferred the cold and unwavering metals of mechanical bodies to that of a squishier flesh form.

In their quest for ripe bodies to pilfer, the robbers manage to recover the body of young woman.

Stone Soul

Still full of colour, her red cheeks stood stiff in a stark contract to her soft blue eyes. The bluest blue you could imagine, a beauty now wasted and doomed to glaze over into a milky void.

Ignoring the lingering thieves, Ish continued digging. He found it to be a hard task, one that could easily earn him a spot beside Sicilla once it was done. But still, he pressed on. He'd honour his daughter, even if it killed him. With no part of her left, the burial of her spares would have to suffice. She wouldn't need them anymore.

Hours of digging passed and he'd only moved a couple of feet of earth. The cold spring dew had hardened every inch of soil, almost giving it the strength of stone. Chilling winds didn't just embolden the dirt, but made the old man's bones creak. It was a losing battle on two fronts, a war he couldn't win.

With a few more feet to go, it was seeming like an overnight job. Sleep didn't wait at his age, and he feared meeting its bounds so far from home: so close to the body thieves. When the rain started spitting down too, things never looked so bleak.

Luckily for Ish, divinity itself came to his aid. His guardian angel made a second appearance. Arriving on the frozen breeze and striding from gravestone to gravestone, the large figure sent the robbers packing in an instant. If Sicilla wasn't deserving of a burial, Ish might have done the same.

"Need some help, sir?" asked Zarpadon. The cloaked mass watched him at a distance, fearing the notion of being shot a second time.

"I've never needed help. Especially from a man of the Order," Ish replied.

"I'm no longer the Order's man, remember. If you don't *need* help, perhaps you'll want it." Zarpadon then held out two objects. One was a pristine shovel, but the other was far more important. In his right hand was a pendant, one Ish had given his child the day she left.

In a shocked stammer, Ish said, "How did you..."

"When you cast me out, I felt lost. My sharp words used to win over so many, years back. But times have changed and my tongue must've dulled over the ages," admitted Zarpadon. "So, I went back to the Casterlands and retrieved this: Sicilla's remains. Now she can have a proper burial."

"This is all that remained of her?" Ish questioned.

"I'm afraid so."

"May I…?"

Taking the pendant in hand, Ish held her close. All that will ever be of her remained in this heart-shaped ruby. The time had come to let her go. With a kiss, he gently planted it in the grave. "Farewell, child."

It didn't take long for them to fill the ground back to shape. Zarpadon's shovelling was far superior to the old man's. But this did raise a curious question from Ish's reluctant mouth.

"Couldn't you just magic this all back to place? Is a mound of dirt really too much for the arcane arts?" asked Ish.

"Not at all, I've seen wizards move mountains," replied the angel. "I do this labour out of penance for my failure. It only seems right."

Ish felt a small sliver of respect wriggling its way back into his mind. Maybe the angel wasn't as ill as he'd once believed?

With the pendant buried, it seemed wasteful to also cast out her spare parts, which Zarpadon had generously lugged back home. When they retreated

back to the store, the clocks had only struck eleven.
Maybe a healthy dose of sleep wasn't so impossible?

"I brought this: an apology." Holding a bottle of red
wine, Zarpadon beheld it with confusion. "I've never
bought intoxicants before. This is a Castern blend. 'A
port sweet as a Castern kiss,' the merchant said.
Vintage, I think. You do drink, don't you?"

Cracking open the aged bottle, Ish accepted alcohol's
place in his life now. Any wounds could be cleansed by
it, both physical and emotional. The angel was right, he
did enjoy the odd tipple once upon a time. But now it
felt like a small sip wasn't going to be enough.

"Many thanks. Care for a glass, Zarp?"

"I'd love to. However, we angels have nothing inside
but crystal. Drinking on an empty stomach is stupid.
Drinking without a stomach? Now that's just
impossible," Zarpadon said light-heartedly.

"Ah, how silly of me. Forgive my ignorance. The tales
make you lot out as all wings and golden halos."
Missing all organic parts, Zarpadon was lucky. With no
heart to ache or brain to race, Ish was jealous.

"We did, for a time. The look was stylish, but the
feathers? They were a mess."

Stone Soul

The port was sour, far more than anything Ish had previously tasted. It'd been years since his last foray into the world of wine, and he blamed the foul flavour on his own bad taste. A few glasses later, the sourness was familiar and he felt a deep peace from it.

"Whoever said this was 'sweet' must lack more taste buds than yourself," Ish grimaced. "I suppose it still gets the job done."

"I apologise. My friend has been known to have poor tastes, both in humour and in wine, it seems," Zarpadon said before trailing off into talks of this and that.

The angel was quite the conversationalist… as long as the receiver was partly hammered. From politics to mechanics, the pair yammered relentlessly. Then, when all seemed over, the angel restated his request.

"Sicilla wasn't just a machine to me. She was a kind *woman*. The only woman to ever make me truly happy," Zarpadon sadly said.

"You and me both. But I think she loved us in different ways," Ish replied, "*I*, a father. You, *a lover?*"

"Oh no, sir. It was never that. She was a friend. I… I was too proud for anything more."

"I know the feeling. My youth was full of pride in the face of romance. Now, all I have is envy of those in love. I'll never see it again and frankly – I won't miss it," smiled the old man, showing his chequerboard teeth.

There had been a few women in Ish's life, and those that were existed far between one another. With no heir to continue his legacy, he didn't have a heaven to look forward to. Heaven was empty to those of solitude.

"There's still time for pride, Ishmael; short thought it may be." Zarpadon's reminder was thick and lay heavy on Ish's soul. "Your girl, she fought for my cause. All I want is to see that cause blossom beyond a fevered dream. I can't let her death be fruitless: it can't be for nothing."

"This world-saving quest…" Ish hesitantly asked. "This quest. Is it a *good* one?"

"The best path to good that I've ever seen."

Honesty was present in the angel's words, it had to. A lie at this point would be both their undoing.

"Then I'll help: for Sicilla."

With a sombre nod, Zarpadon reach into his cloak, withdrawing a roll of tattered scrolls. Stained by dirt and age, the papers were wrecked and their writings illegible. Yet, the diagrams upon the pages looked pristine; great care was placed into preserving them and them alone.

The pictures showed a special clock indeed. Cogs and shrapnel protruded from the malformed device. It closely resembled an apple half mashed to a pulp. Lastly, with an open top fit for an ornate object, the 'clock' would be Ish's greatest challenge yet. "This is too much. A professional mechanist should help, not I."

"We can't do that. My group is splintering from the Order. This means trust runs in short supply now. You're all we have." The angel paused before dropping even more bad news. "I'm afraid you'll need to make this fast. It's needed before next Huiday evening."

"A week! That's insane," Ish gasped as he spat a mouthful of wine across the counter.

"My boss will cover any parts and pieces you'll need. Hells be damned, I'll do all of the leg work. It shouldn't be a problem," assured a now desperate Zarpadon.

Miracles came quick and easy in this city: the Land of Holy Vitality. But to a man of science, miracles weren't a thing you can just 'wish' into existence. A miracle must be earned through many laborious trails. Disheartened, but not dissuaded, Ish remembered his favoured adage.

"Then *fiat*. I'll need a pyrus wielder and several cooling pipes. Oh, and tea, lots of tea."

"I knew you'd be the right choice," cheered Zarpadon. "How does it feel to hold the world on your shoulders?"

Ish did have an answer. Though doing a purposeful act of good, he didn't feel much kinder or nobler. Perhaps the purest of acts didn't always feel pure, but were rather ones free of regret. Because that's what he felt: a notable lack of regret.

Chapter 5: Room 00

Kalsec knew no fear. He was a boy raised with knowledge no other could have. This made him numb to sorrow, but also to happiness. It was a trade off he often questioned the worthiness of. No more so than in the current moment, when faced with a thing of great relief nestled in the arms of something terrifying.

Before him was a thing. A mangled thing that must've once been a man, like he. But this thing was far removed from what a 'man' was. The thing was so deeply consumed by pipes and tubes, it was hard to tell if it was still living. Whatever this person once called itself, it was now an aspect of death, but not given the good grace to die yet.

The man Kalsec looked upon was twisted in the literal sense. His limbs contorted in cardinal directions, arms to the north and west, legs to the south and east. The man's chest was concave and squished all his organs in the shape of an hourglass, pooling at both ends of the torso.

What little remained of the man's skull was malformed from a serious blow. You could barely tell where the wrinkled skin started and the leather bindings ended. All hair and teeth had long gone, save for two sharp and false fangs of silver. If not for such a complex death bed of mechanical torment, the old man would be nothing more than a corpse. More of a corpse than he already was.

The only thing still intact and lucid were the man's eyes. Both were glazing over, but they followed Kalsec's movements with insidious intent. They were two moons gazing down upon the pale boy's lake of sweat.

Whether it was the infected bite or the first genuine fear he'd ever felt, Kalsec was dripping with a stinking smell of weakness. One the old man was quick to notice. With a limp twitch of a crooked nose, the old one coughed out a chuckle.

"Ho ho, that stench takes me back. Welcome, boy." He attempted to wave, but a crack of the wrist was all he could muster. "You'll call me–"

Taking control of the situation and the streak of yellow within, Kalsec interrupted, "I'll call you whatever I please, Zero. I'll call you that as it's all you are to me: nothing."

"Bold words from a brat on death's door," Zero condescended. His words dripped out at a snail's pace and held even less strength than his twisted wrist.

"A rich statement coming from you," Kalsec grinned. "Tell me, does your own stench of urine and almonds fade over time? I may be here a while."

Zero winced and replied, "No. No on both accounts. You'll be done with me soon enough. Just like you'll do away with her downstairs, the ghoulish ingrates, and all those that stand in your way."

The old man was a double dose of mockery and praise, two things that were rarely used together. It was a tough type of admiration, and almost distracted Kalsec from an important question.

"How do you know of Alva? My my, how do you know of the fiends that chased us?" Kalsec asked, caring not for an answer. He only hoped for a word to leave Zero's mouth that wasn't steeped in an enigma or a riddle. "I want answers."

"And you'll get them, one day." Zero's attempt to smile was as twisted as his limbs, an unnatural emotion for the broken bag of bones. Given how malnourished he was, Kalsec assumed him to be some relative of

Alva's. Few pulled off the gaunt and colourless look quite like her. "But for now, you have a job to do."

"You know nothing of my task," Kalsec said as he searched the room for a means to defend himself. At this point he was unsure if he'd need to end two lives or three.

"Of course I do. Your tale is one told by several, these days. You're as unique as that fake accent you tout about the place. Pathetic," Zero said harshly. "And don't give me that–"

Kalsec tried to interrupt Zero for a second time, but only found his voice synchronising with the old man's as they said, *'now you've sealed your fate'*. The matched words were enough to stun Kalsec's tongue, but Zero continued with a further thought.

"–drivel. There's nothing but empty apathy in your words, boy. You care too much of what the world thinks of you. You cannot be the lord you see yourself as. Not now, not with that drivel. You're just a vague stink on the wind."

Never had a mere man dared to call Kalsec out. To mock a crook was a danger, to mock *him* was pure sacrilege. Yet, he could not bring himself to kill Zero, to snuff out the outlier. It was too interesting of a life to take. That, and the infection had begun to drain Kalsec of all remaining strength.

Like a babe begging for a feed, the collapsing Kalsec demanded a solution to his problem.

"I need to be strong. I need to be powerful. It–is–my– destiny," Kalsec cried as he stumbled to Zero's bedside.

"Funny, is it not? How one rogue ghoul can spell your end?" questioned Zero. "Mortality hurts, as I am painfully aware. Given another minute and you'll be lamer than I. As I said: a stink in the wind. But I can help."

The offer came from nowhere and was as unwarranted as Kalsec's own aggressive approach to life. What did Zero have to offer, and did it come at a cost?

"What could you do to help me?" groaned Kalsec. "I doubt your withered claws could stitch my wounds."

"You'll live. I've been bitten more times than I care to admit, back in the day," said Zero. "But times change, and so too does the wind. I could bestow a little gift upon you. One that'll grant you all the power you desire."

By Jack Robinson

When the devil offers you a deal, you'd normally have to think on it, perhaps even sleep on the idea. But Kalsec was out of time to think as an eternal sleep awaited him. Though it was painful, he accepted Zero's help.

With a pant, he indulged the old sage. "Explain."

"Put your faith in god for once," said Zero as he gestured downwards. "Beneath my bed sits the key. A key that opens one's chest to the gift."

"I only have faith in myself," Kalsec assured him as he knelt down and ducked beneath the rusted slats of the bed. With one hand resting on Zero's striped sheets and another feeling for this 'key,' Kalsec's confidence peaked for the second time in one night, and with it came his second downfall.

"Of course you do, and now you'll have to keep that faith in me," replied Zero as the fumbling continued.

There was nothing below but a shimmering streak of reflected light casting a silver shape at the bed's centre. Whilst reaching for it, Kalsec felt its power just from tickling its presence. But its glimmer only sought to distract him.

"What is it?" he asked, breathless.

"A curse. A cursed thing that dooms all who it graces," explained Zero. "Do you accept it?"

As the silver light bent into the shape of a sabre, Kalsec finally felt relief.

"I do," he hypnotically replied.

What followed was a loud array of rapid cracking, then a duo of sharp stabs into the boy's hand, the one left atop the bed. It had happened again: for the second time in one night he'd been bitten. In shock, Kalsec's hand grasped the silver blade with his free hand and shoved it upwards through the thin bedding. A thick black goo slowly dripped down its edge and the fear in the air began to recede with each drop.

Kalsec looked above the bed to see Zero's fangs impaling the boy's hand, the twin teeth piercing through the glove and sunk deep in the flesh. It also appeared that Zero had been impaled by the silver sabre as its point ran straight through his squishy abdomen. A stab for a stab.

With one final exhausted breath, Zero bestowed one final thing to the boy in addition to the gifts of strength and power.

By Jack Robinson

"Dooms all it touches," said Zero with a sadistic smile, one that became immortalised on his face with the gradual onset of rigor mortis. The last thing Zero saw was his reflection dying in Kalsec's eyes.

Withdrawing the sabre and his hand from Zero's jaw, Kalsec became overwhelmed with a great onslaught of feelings. Some were old and others new, but all slowly gnawed at his very being.

At first came a dark cloak of finality to his form. Unlike the heat of his wounds, this was a chilling and empty sense of dread. The reaper's blade was not just in his palm, but also poised around his throat. After tainting the silver shine with both light and dark blood, an invisible pact was sealed. He was locked into the same fate as Zero, only with a delay of an uncertain length.

Next was another burning wave of infection. Every muscle in the boy's back gave up as his heart slowed and his head numbed. So this was what death felt like? Life was the longest thing Kalsec had ever been through, and now it was ending he felt a failure. That was until his last moment came and a final feeling arrived with it.

Lastly, a blast of refreshment flowed into him. It came from Zero's bite and wasted no time charging every fibre with an unending surge of energy. It was as if the boy had slipped from life but didn't have permission to pass. Not a stagnant ghoul like those downstairs, but a different kind of dead. He'd a thirst for blood and it drove him now and forever.

The flood of changes took their toll on his fragile soul, and Kalsec soon found himself collapsing beside Zero. They headed in differing direction, one slipping into oblivion whilst the other gained a new lease on life. One thing they shared was a much-needed rest in a puddle of black blood.

As Kalsec slipped away, he heard the doors of manor crash open below, and Alva's calls as she retreated amidst a calamity of several crashes and bashes.

Not knowing how long he was gone for, Kalsec awoke to the rude insults of Alva as she held back the ghouls, yet again. This time they attempted to breach Room 00 and those within it.

"Good to see you had the time to retire some oldens to the great beyond. Meanwhile I've taken a beating at that fat freak's hand. Wake up!" ordered Alva in a stern voice, no more panicked than her usual tone.

Her body was bruised and bloody, giving her skin a pinkish glow as the fresh cuts leaked a free flow of red. Never had such a macabre sight caught Kalsec's eye with such a lustre. Zero's bite had given him more than an excess of energy, it had given him a real taste for blood.

Stronger and faster than he'd ever felt before, Kalsec saw his now pale reflection in the sheen of his silver sabre. With a grin he accepted his new fate. Though vampirism held him, he'd never felt so alive.

"'Oh, hieratic heathens, bow before your god,'" recited Kalsec as he arose from the puddle. His form was outlined in black ichor which reflected the moonlight that beamed softly through the manor windows. From Alva's eye, all that could be seen was a pair of sharp red eyes engulfed in a cloak of light. "No need to say your prayers, I've got that covered."

In the blink of an eye he pushed Alva aside and with an open palm blasted Room 00's door off its heavy hinges and into the ghouls outside it. Both fat and thin alike were cast far back now the hallway and both lost another limb to such a forceful blow. It was now the undead versus the forever dead, a battle of death and disease.

Using the sabre was like wielding a quill upon a fleshy parchment. The stinking ink eventually spilt from the ghouls and painted the tip of the blade as Kalsec wrote a stanza of suffering on the two. Each rhythmic slash felt so easy, superior to that of his old shoto. After a few more carvings, the ghouls were naught but a mass of chopped meat on the manor's floor, their ooze slowly eating at the wooden boards beneath them.

It was all over too quickly for Kalsec, and he wanted more. The lust lay not in blood alone, but in the fires of ferocity itself. Luckily, a new threat began to present itself.

"My…" Alva gawked with a stunned look that almost split her jaw from her head.

"You should know by now: when I set a goal, I achieve it," lorded Kalsec whilst he wiped the smell off his sabre. "This is the strength I've spent so long seeking. They were doomed the moment my blade grazed them."

By Jack Robinson

Overflowing with a prideful aggression, the boy swung at the room's door frame and punched right through it. He managed to both scare a flinch out of the hardass Alva and send her attention towards the window. Outside stood their next opponents.

"We seem to have drawn some unwanted attention," Alva informed him.

Standing in formation on the manor's lawn was a battalion of paladins, armed to the teeth with swords and shields. Their black iron armour blended into the night sky, and only a few balding heads and golden banners peeked from the darkness. All aside from their pragmatic leader, who was clad with a shiny set of onyx platemail. The blond blademaster held a scroll in hand and was ready to lay down the law.

"Attention, criminal scum. This is Commander Lux, leader of the Old Valour sector of the City Watch–" spoke the onyx leader.

"An overly lengthy title for an overly lengthy ego," Kalsec mocked quietly.

"–you have trespassed on a private residence and committed acts against the laws of the Goddess Bethany." Commander Lux continued for a bit, listing every law to the letter. The slim soldier wouldn't stand a chance against Kalsec. But as for the rest of the battalion? The fledgling monster needed backup. "Surrender peacefully and be met with peace. But continue to terrorise and you'll face only terror."

With a gluttonous look in his eye, Kalsec took Alva's hand and gave her an offer unlike that which Zero did. He offered her a choice.

"What say you, my loyal assistant? Do you die to this man's onyx blade, or do you claim it as your own? I can share my power and make you an avatar of unlimited potential. All I need is a 'yes'."

Caught up in all the temptation vampiric vice brought, Alva slowly nodded with a glazed stare.

"Very well," Kalsec said as he opened wide.

They shared a kiss that was more passionate than most, though passion of a whole other kind. As his fangs nipped her lower lip, she only tightened her grasp and the black blood flowed freely from master to apprentice. When the deed was done, they both held blood on their tongue and a sensation that could only be described as orgasmic. While Alva drifted into the

same sleepy state he had just risen from, the
Commander grew impatient.

"Criminal scum, you have one minute to comply
before my men send you to the Goddess' judgement,"
Lux called.

With his sabre once again shining in the moonlight,
the time for further chaos had come. Given Alva
needed another moment before waking, Kalsec would
have to start the next dance of death on his own.

Bursting from the manor's window he drew his
blade and dove for the unprepared Commander.
Landing a single slice on Lux's cheek was all he needed.

With a grand pose, Kalsec let the doomed
commander know, "Now you've sealed your fate."

***

"That is the story behind this beauty," Kalsec told
Syphus. "A tale I hope more than earns its worth,
wouldn't you say?"

The masked man's eyes lit up with a proud warmth.
He was quick to answer, slinging a dozen follow up
questions towards the boy. It was nothing suspicious,

just where he'd been since and what he did. In the five years since becoming a vampire, time had seemed rather inconsequential for Kalsec. He didn't age as fast and didn't need to sleep each and every night. Everything was a blur of red and black.

"Oh, you know," Kalsec said nonchalantly, "I ended some more ghastly ghouls, joined a gang, killed some people, betrayed the gang, betrayed Alva and then tried to end her. The usual, really."

Syphus looked at him with a drought of respect. He felt pride, but not the good kind, the guilty sort.

"You're a wretched thing," Syphus said. "You're a monster, and I *love* it."

"If that's what charges your wand, then so be it. I care not for the admiration of lesser men," Kalsec shrugged. With each man he felled his soul shed and became that much smaller, while his ego fed on the shed scraps like a ravenous worm through soil. "Do you want to purchase this blade or not?"

Since executing Zero in the cold moonlight, the sabre had adopted a name befitting a midnight murder. The Moonsabre was a sentimental piece in Kalsec's heart, a piece he must purge. Selling the sabre to a collector was the best way to crush sentiment and grind it into a fine stack of wealth.

No one knew where Syphus truly heralded from, a masked man with no past beyond his time in service to a northern king. The cloaked collector was known for seeking unholy artefacts from around the lands. If he wouldn't buy the Moonsabre, then no one would.

However, the man offered no coin or jewel for the silver prize: he only bartered in words. A form of currency older than any other, secrets and rumours held a timeless value that Kalsec could appreciate. An invaluable income for a man without a notion of time.

"Entrust the blade to my hand and I'll give you a name," Syphus offered. Betwixt the man's fingers was a slip of parchment, likely a lead to something legendary. In the northern king's court, Syphus had a penchant for information and the avarice it seeded in the mind.

It was easy to hold greed for monetary wealth, but impossible to refuse the call of revelation. For every truth he learned, the world became that much smaller, easier to grasp in his palm. A goal both he and Syphus strove for. "This name will tug on fate's string and pull you closer to your heart's desires."

"A tempting offer. But I doubt you know of my desires," Kalsec replied.

"I know you better than you know yourself, whelp. Remember, it's my job," Syphus said with a subtle air of intimidation. "I know you seek that which is broken. I know you want to face the sun once more. I know you didn't betray Alva. She, in fact, betrayed you."

The man stood up and leaned over the table with a calm demeanour, yet he cast such a verbal shadow that everyone in the inn perked up their ears. "I know these things because I am a man of manifest. When I seek a prize, I claim it without delay. Yes, it is *I* that found this parchment for you. A gift meant to set you on the 'right path,' a road that will enviably lead you to becoming a man of manifest like I. It is destiny for the *extra ordinary* to be extraordinary. You will accept my offer as it is written in the stars and etched in the very annals of Prime. As I said, it-is-inevitable. You know?"

A chill held the inn hostage. Each nape tingled and every hair was set on edge. Even Kalsec's dead form felt the cold. Before he knew it, the sabre was in Syphus' hand and the deal was practically done.

Silence continued as the two stared each other down. Both looked as if they could end the other, but really neither could, not yet.

"A man of manifest indeed," Kalsec agreed as he released the blade into Syphus' care.

Without uttering another word, Syphus slipped the parchment in Kalsec's now empty palm and took his leave. Like the wind had carried him away with it, the collector left as quickly as the chill he cast.

All Kalsec was left with was a thin piece of paper with a single name upon it. As he opened the folded object of fate, he could only wonder what name could change his long life. Another friend of Syphus' perhaps? Maybe another king or lord? Imagine the buyer's remorse when it was neither.

'Edgar Svanold' read the parchment.

<u>Chapter 6: Wine and Whiners</u>

Philip felt like a devious devil. It wasn't an ill-fitting description: he did indeed betray the Warden's confidence for personal gain, but the look didn't sit right on him. He often looked up to better men for stoic guidance. Though he'd never really met any of these men in the flesh, their legends spoke far more for them than a real meeting ever could.

Now, mimicking the classic 'two birds, one bolt,' technique, Philip sought out Donsis Allisteel. An elven toff with more wealth than wisdom, Donsis was known as a fearsome money loaner in the city. Several social circles called him a 'cut-throat collector,' but from the Order's files it was clear the elf was nothing more than a hooplehead projecting a visage of viciousness.

No man or woman that crossed paths with Donsis ever lost their lives, only their money. If he was as cut-throat as the rumour said, then he was rather clean about it. Still, even a faux reputation was something to be wary of, and Philip strode down Andover Avenue with a cautious gait.

By Jack Robinson

The Miracle Mile was colder than usual tonight.
What was a place lined with old warehouses and grain
stores for the Order usually made for a long road of
tired workers and a bevy of vendors selling barely-
edible snacks to them. But tonight there was nothing,
no life and no sour stench of ankhi broth. All Philip
could see or feel was a thick layer of fog and the uneasy
feelings hidden within it.

Though the Warden expected him to search the
entire avenue, Philip knew exactly where to look. It was
one of his and Hericore's agents that had tipped Donsis
off to the Order's imminent seizure of his property and
freedom. It was also the same agent that followed
Donsis after.

Sitting comfortably behind a rendering factory,
hidden from sight and smell, was a far less odorous
building. It was an old storage warehouse meant to
hold thousands of items ready for distribution by
wagon or courier.

Elliott Elixirs was the name of the company that once
owned this place, a group so long gone that Philip
couldn't remember a world with them in it. To see the

end result of a failed venture just showed the costs of losing if he failed his own mission.

Keeping a calm hand, Philip grasped the gates to the warehouse and pulled them apart gently, so as to not betray the element of surprise. Donsis had fled alone, but this didn't mean he was still alone.

Agility was a trait of few men these days. In a world of towering knights in the north, clanking war machines in the south and savage tribals in between, it was rare to exercise a little restraint and serve a small slice of delicacy at the war table. However, it quickly became apparent that Donsis was not the delicate sort.

A loud bout of angry pacing was heard through the cracks in the building's mortar. Inside was the elf, cocooned in a womb of woe. He argued with himself in mumbled words, exposing his hiding spot to any wanderer with a working pair of ears.

The flicker of a dim string of half-melted candles lit the large warehouse and Philip's eye alike as he spied on the cranky criminal. All that inhabited the empty stretch of stone and steel were a couple of crates, a makeshift tent, and a hamper of partly-eaten provisions. All an elf needed to lie low for a few months.

'*The cost of infamy,*' thought Philip as he scoffed at the tiny holding. The Order had seized over eighty-thousand roths worth of goods from Donsis' now abandoned home, not to mention the cost of the home itself. Philip wondered if the poor fool had anything left, pride and dignity included.

It was money more than anything Philip sought from the sallow-skinned geek. It would be a shame to waste an evening chasing an empty dream; even if he'd been doing so for the past few months.

As expected of a warehouse, the room was floored in two layers, an upper entrance of stone only a few steps above a sunken surface of wooden planks. They seemed like an architectural depiction of Etheriam and Tarus: heaven and hell. Above was a grey floor of perfectly fitting stone bricks, while below was a wasteland of shoddily placed and rotted oak planks. It was on this lower layer that the elf resided.

Like all elves, Donsis was a frame of sickly yellow skin upon a skeletal form. With gangly arms that stretched to their ankles and a lack of cheek mass, elves' only redeeming quality were a pair of deep purple eyes. Protruding and round, they glimmered like imperial eggs and held an infinite depth to them.

Eventually, the elf's bulbous eyes met with Philip's narrowed gaze. Surprise was no longer a privilege for the courier, and the time to preform was upon him once again. The elf seemed uneasy at the gaze, jumping in his sickly skin. Perhaps a softer mask would be needed with Donsis?

"Hey, you!" called the elf. "What're you doing out there?"

With the most innocent voice he could muster, Philip replied, "Looking for you, Mr. Allisteel. I'm a retainer of yours, my man."

A long pause followed. It was one of misjudged intentions that almost ended both of their wits. Both believed the other to be dangerous, and neither wanted to make the next move.

"A–A retainer? What are you… um retaining?" asked Donsis. The elf slowly moved behind a crate. "Are you the 'Siren Bedder' that Cassidy's sending?"

'*I was going to say courier, but…*' Philip thought with a sly smirk. With a title like 'Siren Bedder' involved, the opportunity to try on a new persona was too good to pass up. If Donsis was looking for a man working for this 'Cassidy' person then Philip was the guy.

"Of course," fibbed Philip. "Cass said you'd be hiding somewhere. Had to be sure this wasn't some old shanty for beggars. Lotta fiends about these days. Ya never know who to trust."

A second silence broke out. This one was less hostile but twice as awkward.

"Could ya open the door for me?" Philip asked.

"Oh," Donsis said with realisation. "*Eine moment bitte.*"

Elvish was an old tongue, aged beyond any record the history books cared to keep. Often seen as too good for human tongues, Philip dared not learn it in any form. All he needed were the words of the common language and those of his homeland. One to situate him in the present and the other to act as a bitter reminder of the past.

Donsis opened the lock with a shaky hand and rattled it free from a rusty grip. With a small gesture of open arms he invited Philip into his world. A world of stagnant and medicinal air. Likely a holdover from its days as Elliott Elixirs. As the boy examined the hollow structure, Donsis clasped his hands together and gave an expectant look.

"So?" Donsis wondered.

The elf wanted an answer to something, an answer that Cassidy's real worker would likely know. Without a confident response in mind, Philip just shook his head limply.

"Oh, brilliant," groaned Donsis. "So it can't be built? Wonderful. Can I go now?"

"No!" snapped Philip in a desperate attempt to keep things on track. "I'm a bit of a slow-in-the-mind. All of my gears don't spin at once, an all. Why don't you explain to me about this thing what needs to be built."

"That was Cassidy's job," Donsis said with a suspecting stare.

"And she did. But like I say, I be a little slow," Philip said. Hoping the lie would stick, he crept a hand behind his back just in case it didn't. Passing the first minute with a stranger was always the hardest and his dagger would be a helpful tool in pushing passed such a hard time. "Cass said you were the brains of the deal, after all."

"She did?" smiled Donsis as his ill face lit up. "Oh, she did."

"I have the building smarts, but you – my good sir – are the street smarts." Philip could barely stand being so brown-nosed. This went double when praising a person of minimal moral fortitude. Animals shouldn't need to be coerced with words: a simple bit of bribery usually sufficed.

Donsis was no ordinary animal, however. He was a special breed. A beast so clean he could be mistaken for a civil creature. An act that fooled nearly all, even Donsis himself. Yet, regardless of his clean image, the brain of a savage still belonged to him. Philip concluded, "So explain away and let us proceed."

"All righty then," Donsis said sheepishly. The elf rummaged through a stack of notes within one of the crates. Eventually, he produced a hand-drawn layout of the warehouse and another of a tunnel held high by beams of steel. "My partners in crime have devised a way to please both our needs. Mine and theirs, that is."

"I've not seen these before," Philip said. He told the first truth of the night, followed shortly by another lie. "Must've been swapped in the mail with this…"

With an expression and pose reminiscent of last week's opera, Philip displayed the scarlet letter with grandeur. 'Twas an act that was lost to ignorance as Donsis failed to look or listen. The elf remained with his celestial eyes locked on the drawings.

"Cass wants a way into the city, and I need one out. I'm willing to pay you for what I'm told is a rather easy bit of shadow construction? A three mile long tunnel that runs beneath Valordolt's sewers and wall, both. Done without the Order suspecting a thing," Donsis explained.

"Very well, can do. Ya know I'm not a frickin' miracle man, right? A three mile tunnel?" Philip said, losing himself in the scale of the request. A request not even meant for him, yet still a massive one that blew the mind. "All that to smuggle out little ol' you? You know what, sure, whatever. Back on track: I had this letter show up instead of my own plans. *Maaaybe* it was meant for you?"

For a second time Philip presented the note and was met with an unexpected response. Donsis pulled his own red letter from his pocket and held it in a similar manner. It was unmistakably a brother to the one Philip held, an origami shaped like a mouse and a virgin wax seal holding it all together.

With a look of genuine shock, Philip asked, "How did you get that letter, sir?"

As the courier of these letters, Philip couldn't recount this one's existence. If secret notes were being passed around, then Donsis may not be the only rat in Philip's life. The boy wasn't mad at this news, being more impressed than anything.

"Watch your tone, brat," Donsis snapped, sensing a change in the wind and a chance to dominate their talk like any good coward would do. "I've enjoyed you so far. But I'm the elf in the room, and don't forget that."

After pulling a familiar opened bottle of port from the crate, the elf recounted the origins of the letter. The cold air seeped into the room and onto Philip's brow, summoning a fearful sweat. He'd left the Warden's gift in the hands of some bum, a tale only Hericore and Zarpadon knew of.

"If the story of the letter is important to you, which it shouldn't be, I'll happily tell its tale," Donsis smirked and showed off a row of near perfect teeth, mired by a thin coat of yellow. "It all started way back when, in the mythical period known as last week."

The story continued and failed to reveal anything other than the elf's terrible narrator voice. It was a letter that appeared with the bottle one night on the doorstep of the warehouse. However, with each painfully dull sentence Donsis spoke, the anger in Philip rose. He longed to know the content of the letter and the high and mighty elf wasn't sharing.

In time, another feeling of intuition and instinct took over the boy. Never had he ever wanted to hurt someone so bad in all his life. Well, at least in the last few months.

"Enough of the babbling, Donsis. You want me to start building? Think again. I'm not acting as some slack-jawed cur a moment longer. If you want to hear *my* truth then you'll read me that letter right now," demanded Philip, forgetting the rumoured danger of the dodgy debtor.

"Excuse me?" Donsis replied. Though he hollered this back, it was done with a cracking voice of a fearful creature. Along with a small step back the elf added, "I have powerful friends, you know? My cousin Yikii would–"

"Powerful friends? You should check out your enemies. The Warden's got the Order's best on your hide," Philip threatened. Without realising, he was holding his cobalt dagger in hand opposite to his red letter. "Now give me the damn letter!"

Philip didn't know what to expect, but the result was an interesting one as Donsis immediately turned tail and ran from the tiny blade. It seemed the stories of the elf's vicious nature were only *'slightly'* exaggerated.

Fate favoured Philip further as the elf's escape was a short-lived one. Within a few nervous steps, the chicken tripped over one of the loose floorboards, which sent him flying head-first onto the stone steps that followed. With a loud squawk, Donsis' downfall was accompanied by small fountain of blood.

"Urghowww gowds!" mumbled Donsis through a thick coat of crimson and a faceful of brick. "My jaaw."

"Fortune favours the bold," Philip smirked. "I suppose that applies to both the good and the bad kind."

The boy wasn't without soul and moved to help the elf from his compromised position. On approach, a now disoriented Donsis crawled away as his ego melted into a puddle of piss beneath him. All talk of supremacy and importance disappeared and Donsis was only left with a beggar's tongue.

"St–stay back. I'll give you the cursed letter. Just don't bring any of your sour luck any closer," pled Donsis, now backed up to the building's wall. "Cassidy needs my coin, an–and they can't have it whilst I rot."

"How about a trade then?" Philip held out a stretch of cloth from his breast pocket. "Some clotting for your nose in exchange for a piece of clotting for my eyes?" As Donsis pulled out his shaking palms for the trade, Philip held them tight. Though the sweat made things difficult the boy made sure to add one little order to his initial terms. "Don't move either. I'll have question on its subject matter."

Once unfolded the letter was addressed not to Donsis, but to Philip himself. In the same font and colour as the usual scarlet notes, it read:

Philip,

By Jack Robinson

Assuming you haven't smacked it over the elf's head
there's a special bottle of wine in his possession meant
for an old angel acquaintance of ours. Make sure he
gets it by the week's end. You'll thank me later.

-H

Suddenly, things became far clearer for Philip. The
letter was no act of betrayal, but one of secret
instruction. Once again, he needed to kill two birds
with one bolt. After checking his watch, the boy
smirked at Donsis who now lay unconscious at the
sight of his own blood.

The elf was no bastion of strength, but even this was
below the standards of the world's weakest wretches.
Yet it just made Philip's move all the easier. The world
had a weird way of making the simple tasks even
simpler for the lucky lad.

"I'm afraid I've been untruthful with you, vermin,"
he said to Donsis' unresponsive form. "I was sent here
by the good Warden to retrieve you. I don't know a
Cassidy and I hope to god I never do. A three mile
tunnel, seriously?"

Reclaiming his now stained pocket cloth, Philip used it to tie the elf's hands to his feet. Escape would prove difficult while Philip would send for back up. For a moment he wondered if the Warden was the right man to send for. Perhaps this Cassidy would pay a handsome bounty. Then again, even Philip doubted this level of lucky foresight.

"Sit tight, Donsis," he said. "You'll be in irons by sun up and I'll be one step closer to achieving Hericore's plans."

Before leaving, he spied the wine bottle sitting innocently atop the crate. Remembering the scarlet letter, the boy nabbed the bottle before the Order arrived. "*My* plans," he corrected.

***

As predicted, the Warden, backed by a handful of armoured men, raided the hollow remains of Elliot Elixirs. The minimal spoils became property of the Order and its Warden: some roths, paper bonds, and what caught Philip's eye – a bagful of gemstones.

By Jack Robinson

There were about a dozen stones in total, and they were a mixture of everything from clean cut emeralds to splendid sapphires to a single fiery ruby. He didn't know why they caught his eye over the others, but Philip knew he *had* to have them.

When the Warden began to count the gems away from the greedy gaze of his paladin guards, Philip came in close and resumed his former charm from the opera. Like a little pup longing for a treat, he ogled the gems and asked a bold question.

"May I dip my hand in the cookie jar? As a show of good faith?" Philip asked. "I often dream of having a few stones in hand. It seems my fate is tied to them."

Looking through him with a similar stare of avarice, the Warden turned him down.

"It was my understanding that helping your mental mate was a 'show of faith?'" said the Warden. "Besides, these stones are meant for the Order's coffers, not mine."

Denied what he saw as rightfully his, something in Philip got the better of him again as the mask slipped an inch. Another gut instinct perhaps, or simply the tug of want?

"Don't play the noble one here, Percival. Everyone from Valordolt to the Castern borders knows of your past. You can slip a little lie pass a rube, but never one as big as this. I'd be deaf or dumb to believe that a former bandit turned law man wouldn't have a little stash on the side, aye? So stop being what you're not and tip me a trio of gems, *sir*," mocked the boy.

Philip's schemes often ran away with him. His wealth of instinct was always a fleeting thing and often led him into swimming troubled waters. This was a fact reinforced by the Warden's strict response. A swift punch to the gut was never so badly required.

"Listen here, boy," the Warden whispered while holding Philip by the scruff of his neck. "If we're in business, we need to establish a little pecking order, see? You might've struck a well of fear in Donsis' belly, but don't presume every man is the same. You're his better, as I am yours. Got it?"

Upon release, Philip rubbed his now red raw neck and gave a look of forced acceptance on his face which matched in colour. With a begrudging nod, Philip bit his lip and allowed the Warden to leave unimpeded.

By Jack Robinson

"Oh, and remember this," continued the Warden. "I don't embezzle, from criminals or otherwise. You'd have to check your master's books for that. I've lightened my moral compass over the years whilst he, and *several* others, have sought to snuff theirs. Such is life."

As the Warden left with a sombre whistle, Philip was stuck with a sour feeling. Yes, he'd achieved his goals of both Hericore and the scarlet letter. However, without a lick of reward from anyone aside from a bottle of tainted wine, he was left dissatisfied. Most things lacked proper reward in these times, and he'd grown accustom to let down.

All the Order had left him with was the lone and dirty bottle of port, the source of tonight's contention. Taking the drink in hand, the boy almost slipped from its sweet lips before remembering what that would entail.

With a bitter smile on his face, Philip looked to the future and all it contained. He saw himself standing atop the world with a matching expression to his current one. Victory without reward.

Chapter 7: Wight Wail

Ish's week passed and the store remained closed. The cobwebs expanded at a rapid rate; spiders were soon to owe him a hefty amount of rent and he'd need it. His job was no longer of concern now he had some real work to do.

Work wasn't as bad as his hygiene, which faltered even further. If not for the spiders a swarm of flies would surely infest the repugnant air. Coughs and wheezes also arose in Ish's chest. From cold lungs, he'd spew forth a handful of phlegm per day. Health, much like hygiene, mattered little to him. Times were changing and so was he.

The last day of the week was always the slowest. Six hours of planning resulted in only three of execution. Ripping apart Sicilla's replacement, Ish finalised the 'clock' with some recycled pieces. After a few more tweaks it was finally completed. What a marvel he had created.

The aged blueprints held a single line of legible text the name 'Quartz Lock'. Ish could only speculate on its purpose, let alone Zarpadon's intentions with such a device.

Its pulped apple body gave way to a dozen mechanisms within, and still, you could hold this petite beauty in the palm of your hand. The cogs whirled with a harsh grind, but complemented the shrill chime of its varied bells and whistles.

The brass and bronze enigma was soon to be claimed by Zarpadon, another enigma who would arrive any minute now. But before the angel's return came the time for some final touches. Inscribing Sicilla's name upon the Quartz's base, Ish made a smile so big it pushed half his moustache into his nostrils.

"One last run, kid," he said. Four knocks struck the door, meaning only one thing. "It's unlocked!"

"What about Don's men? I could've been a thieving hooligan," said Zarpadon as he slowly crept into sight.

Something was wrong with the angel, and had been for a couple of days. Each morning the two would meet, share another bottle of red, and plan out the next piece of the Quartz Lock. Zarpadon would gather the parts, and Ish would snap them together. However, what started off as mornings of conversation soon turned to long quiet slogs. A heavy burden weighed on his new friend's face and he didn't know why.

Today's meeting never even happened. All Ish received was a box of unnecessary parts and an opened bottle of grimy port, sweet thought it was. The package was rushed and uneasy, all tied together with a ruffled red note. Something was eating at Zarpadon and he didn't know what.

"Those brats wouldn't bother me – not after the whole neighbourhood heard me shoot you," Ish joked.

Emotion did appear often in the angel's words. But in a blander tone than usual, he replied, "Again, thanks for that."

They stood in silence for a piece, but importance overcame pleasure. Ish held the Quartz up to his guardian angel and expected the sad air to clear. But life was never that easy.

"Come with me, Ishmael." This was an order, and it was the sternest one to ever leave Zarpadon's mouth. "My boss wants to congratulate you in person."

"You're sounding rather demanding tonight. This is a joyous day." Replying with a short 'hrmph', Zarpadon took the Quartz in one hand and Ish in the other.

Soon enough, after traversing half the city, they ended up in the Market District. For years the district had been a large stretch of commercial land snaking its way around several other parts of Valordolt, hidden below the greater districts above. It slid between the hardy core of the Order's cathedral and the gloomy prison with precision. The Market District acted as a perfect no man's land for the two, sunken deep within the cracks of the city.

"This place has seen better days," Ish groaned. His comment came at the sight of dried pools of blood, still carrying a faint stench. The pools existed in only one place: outside an abandoned pet store. Why they came here was unknown, and given the situation, he was growing more afraid to ask.

Stepping into the building, Ish felt better about the state of his own shop. The discord strewn about this place was twice the level of his, and a deep joy was found in being the least trashy. However, his angel companion didn't reach a similar place of pleasure.

"Listen, Ishmael, I need to be truthful with you," levelled Zarpadon.

"If it's about my payment, I don't mind. Building this thing was reward enough," Ish said, absorbed by the thrill of creation.

Zarpadon turned away and said, "No. I'm afraid it's worse. Far worse."

Taking a fragmented jewel from beneath his cloak, the angel gently placed the ruined prize atop the Quartz, sending the machine wild with spinning parts and clicking pieces.

Ish adjusted his spectacles and found himself struck by awe. "Amazing. In all my life I've longed to see a device so complex. Here I stand, as its creator."

"'Tis a sight. But you need to understand, I didn't know anything about this before Viday."

"Anything about *what*, exactly?" Worry sprouted within Ish's heart and his friend shared the feeling.

Moving down into the depths of the store, they arrived at a hideaway. Tidy, but tight, the hideout presented crates of goods and empty cages all around the lengthy room. What must've been a warehouse for the store was now a meeting place for all of Zarpadon's pals.

By Jack Robinson

The basement looked far cleaner than above, free from the last owner's bloody mess. Decorating the room were banners of a red dragon with weak, yellow eyes.

"Welcome to my home. The base of the Drakeguard Knights," Zarpadon said.

"Zarp, this is a wee bit creepy," Ish cautionously replied. A pause swept the room, before bad news found him again.

A pair of recently familiar, weak and yellow eyes peeked from shadows at the room's end. The fabled drake hid in the dark, guarded by an abyss. Scared though he was, Ish stepped forward and faced the drake head on.

"You must be the boss. It's a pleasure." With a bow, Ish quivered in place. Never had he left the walls of the Valordolt, meaning he'd never crossed paths with such a beast in the wild. Whatever was to follow terrified his very core.

The drake didn't answer. His yellow eyes turned sad as only a sigh left his beak. If the shadows were lifted, Ish would even see the beast shed a tear.

"You never said he was polite," the drake said, in a wizened voice, bestowing gentle tones. "Why must fate always make it so difficult?"

"What does he mean, Zarp?" Ish wondered.

"Like I said, we only found out a few days back," sighed the angel, "There's one last task we need from you, Ishmael."

Dedicated to seeing Sicilla's final wishes fulfilled, Ish quickly replied, "Okay. I'll do it."

More silence followed.

"You may want to reconsider," the drake said.

Zarpadon placed the Quartz Lock on a create between them and the drake. The whirling slowed, as did the beats of Ish's own aged heart.

"For our plan to work: to create a miracle capable of saving this planet… We have to make a *payment*."

The word 'payment' was said with such shame, Ish had a good idea of the consequences.

"A payment in blood? You want my blood." The others shook their heads, giving the impression of more. "You want my life?!"

"Time is short, too short. All over the planet, time is collapsing. We need to *give* time to *make* time. All your remaining years will be used up, and in return, the universe will stabilise… for now," the drake explained.

"For now!? What does that even mean? How much would my short life even give?" Ish babbled.

"Enough!" Zarpadon silenced Ish, still unable to look in his direction.

Ish crystal friend turned from optimistic to stone-faced in an instant. This was a fake front and neither of them *wanted* this to happen. Yet, both of them understood it *needed* to.

"Zarpadon, please, don't force this. I'll do it in his stead," the drake interrupted.

"No, boss, you know the rules. If you do it then we're all dead," denied Zarpadon.

All this talk of time and rules was too much for Ish. As a basic man, he had basic goals, and thus only knew of basic things. The Drakeguard argued for a bit, clouding the air with angered talks of sacrifice. Amongst it all, Ish heard Sicilla's voice echoing on the wind. She was all that mattered to him, past and present, living and dead. If she had trusted the Guard's goals, then she'd want this too. A sacrifice needed to be made, and he needed to be with his child again. A dark trade with lighter results.

"Time's running short, boys. *Stop – arguing,*" Ish demanded. Thinking of what would become of him after death was a concept rarely taken on, even at his age. A rage of red and blue mixed inside, causing anger and sadness to both belt out in his words. His cheeks went red and were trickling with a few tears; the regret had finally arrived. "If my life will save this land? Then, *fiat*. Let it be done! I'm not a man who will be missed, so what does it matter?"

"Mr. Peacock…" admired the drake, speechless in the wake of his generosity.

"I'm sorry," added Zarpadon. The angel rested his heavy mitt upon Ish's shoulder and added, "You will be missed. I'll hold you name above all else, once this is over."

"Don't! My name was never meant for statues and songs. A tombstone will do me just fine," Ish smiled sombrely. He stepped up to the Quartz and placed his wrinkled hands onto the device. "How does this work, anyhow?" Gesturing a finger across his crystal neck,

Zarpadon made it pretty clear. "If I'm to die, make it quick."

The humble clockmaker had never pondered his end, unlike any others that lived past their prime, but Ish still had always one final wish for the inevitable moment. Wanting to die surrounded by family, Ish had achieved this in a rather obtuse way.

"That I can promise. One warm buzz is all you'll feel," Zarpadon said.

After a moment of hesitation, the angel refused his duty. Quaking with guilt, he withdrew and regretfully said, "I can't. I could reduce a dozen criminals to ash, but not one innocent. Definitely not a friend."

Nothing happened for a time. All three were too overcome by awkwardness to forge a single word or action. Ish was ready, but neither of his allies were willing. After a night like this, was he expected to live?

Something had to give. In the end it was neither party who surrendered to the dark deed. Rather an unexpected third party took the burden.

A stabbing pain struck Ish in the chest. His lungs squeezed together, compressing his heart and juicing it of blood. Death – much like time – waited for no one, especially old men. Coughing and spluttering like a clogged machine, it was all ending faster than anyone expected.

"What's happening?" Zarpadon said in shock, cradling Ish's seizing body.

Waves of needle-like pain crashed across Ish's surface as he cried out in pain. It was the perfect storm of agony. A balance of swiftness and suffering.

"Philip…" sighed the drake. "It must be."

"No," Zarpadon denied, shaking his head feverishly. "He couldn't. He doesn't have it in him, like you or I."

"Then how else? No limits exist for boy that longs to become a man." Hericore lamented his accusation before adding, "Still, he had the gall to do what we could not. It was a bitter thing too. Much like his wine, I'm sure."

The pains contracted faster and with greater strength. Ish's words were limited to the amount of breaths he'd left. Just one.

"Sicilla…"

As Ish's life faded away, the Quartz fired up, bells and whistles ablaze. Things seemed to end slower, but painlessly. At the end of the end, a good end is all you can ask for. Euthanasia, with a cause.

Letting the oceans of heaven wash him away, Ish got his wish. As he ascended to what lied beyond, Sicilla was waiting for him. A good end.

Epilogue

Hericore's beak trembled. He couldn't tell if it was guilt or pestilence that was causing the jitter, and he was afraid to know. The truth would only lead to further upset, and at that moment, he felt as though his heart could bear no more.

Despair took its toll on the heart, and aged hearts more than others. After a life of sacrifice, Hericore had now stooped to throwing others in the fire instead. Ish had only know the Arch-Paladin for a moment, and what an impression Hericore must've left. Did Ish's final breaths hold malice or mercy?

It was clear he wasn't the only one steeped in regret. Zarpadon showed no feeling, he couldn't, but it was obvious he was mired with angst. Even an angel could feel like a demon, and even forgiveness couldn't wash away the newest stain on their honour.

The two both hoped for the ends to provide justice for the means and provocation for their future resolve. They acted as if it was their own lives now cast aside. They grieved for a man who had died without a sign of grief.

However, once this man began to pass away, another stepped into the room and took his place. Philip had returned with a lackadaisical look on his face and pep in his step. Now was not the time for joy, even if it was made with oblivious cause.

The boy danced down the stairs into the darkness below. He was happily descending into the horror with no clue of what part he played in its existence. At least Hericore hoped as much.

It was clear someone had poisoned Ish's last drink with something foul. Given the shock both he and Zarpadon shared, it left room for only one present suspect. It didn't take long for Philip to confess either.

"Ah, you're done with the dirty deeds," Philip said as he checked his watch. "One 'time device' good to go on time. Well, with a minute to spare."

As the boy glided across the room, he made sure to step carefully over Ish's rapidly drying out husk. It was no secret of his involvement with Ish's death. It was a fact Philip almost seemed to relish in, like a child waiting on a treat for a chore well done.

"You dare?" seethed Zarpadon.

"I do," replied Philip as he stood side by side with the crystal being. "It had to be done, Zarpy. You know that and clearly so does Her–"

Before he could finish, Zarpadon landed a lightning fast blow to the boy's cheek. It was made with a forceful wave of arcane power behind it. It was a blow so large that it sent Philip spinning to the floor. Though forceful, it left little damage; calculated for optimal pain and minimal scarring.

"I said: don't you *fucking* dare, Philip. Murderer, fiend, smug waste of flesh!" Zarpadon cried out as his crystal body glowed with a deep pink hue of arcanic rage. "He was – he was…"

"I deserved that," groaned Philip, adjusting his jaw and nose the best he could. "Ah! That stings."

"Be glad I don't send you up with him. Though I doubt heaven awaits you," Zarpadon threatened. "I doubt it awaits any of us."

Hericore was unfortunately on the side of deceit here. For once, Philip's heated head had saved them from defeat at the hands of their own morality. If Ish hadn't died then the Quartz Lock would never work, and their plans would cease.

By Jack Robinson

It didn't take long for Zarpadon's rage to dim. Anger didn't come often to the angel and that also meant holding a grudge was difficult. It was likely the only thing sparing Philip from further punishment. But Hericore couldn't chance another life on a 'likely' theory.

"He's right, Zarpadon. What he did was dark, but a darkness we all sought to bring about. Even Ish was willing," Hericore conceded.

Picking a side always left at least one man wanting, but ultimately it needed to be done. Respect came from resolve, while resolve came from decision. Zarpadon's respect was clear, even through his lingering anger.

"Did it have to be so *violent*?" asked Zarpadon.

"No. But options were limited in the time we had. I suppose we've been putting off the inevitable. We'll pay for this act, all of us, one way or another." Hericore gave Ish another look and winced. "But we all knew what was at stake if we hesitated. Well done, Philip. You were harsh, but swift in your actions."

The boy gave a warm look beneath his pained face. Hericore added, "But don't think of this a 'good' deed. I can only imagine how much this scheme burdened you."

"My scheme?" Philip asked.

"Poisoning Ish's wine," Zarpadon clarified. "We are no fools here. All except you, maybe."

Philip gave a glimpse of confusion before a wash of realisation dripped from every pore of his body.

"Big words from a big man. Yet it was you that wanted to put the man to peace in the first place," replied Philip. "Do you really think he's resting with Sicilla now?"

"I can only hope," Zarpadon said with a slouch. "'Lest this world be a cruel one: devoid of fairness."

"Very well," Philip placed out his hand. "Truce? I overstepped my bounds, but only to achieve what you could not. That fair enough for ya?"

Zarpadon refused and turned away, torn between acceptance and angst. Hericore didn't act so callously and wrapped his still shaking claw around Philip's bone dry mitt. They shook to a kinder future and a clean operation thence forth.

With half the room at peace, it was time to return to schedule. Things around them had almost completely ground to a halt. The candlelight waved no more, the flies buzzed no more, the world of Magnus was becoming stiff. All except the trio and their agents.

"Now, I don't long to see you two make up. I just need you to rally the Guard and make sure the time Ish has bought us isn't wasted in vain. You have your orders, now let's get to work," Hericore ordered.

"All right!" Philip cheered. "Krell's been working with the Warden for near a week now. He'll re-aquire the elf for us. I'll snag the mad dog, Kenneth. I wanna peek into the mind of that mystery."

With another dancing march, Philip promptly left before imparting some final condolences. "Cheer up, boss. We've got a world to save," he said with a wink.

This left Hericore alone with Zarpadon and the twitching husk of their newest sin. Both longed for an easier solution, but they were glad to be rid of the problem. One of many.

"Is this truly going to save us? This plan of ours?" Zarpadon asked as he left.

"Us? No," Hericore frowned.

Understanding, Zarpadon nodded before setting off. "I'll get the 'new fish', then. I best take my time. Else I'll ended up ruining Philip's face for real tonight, that freak. Keep an eye on him, sir. He never seems to scar or bruise. Never effected by the consequences of his actions."

Once alone, Hericore let a load off as he collapsed exhausted into a pile of dust and junk. The ordeal had drained what little stamina he still retained. A year of illness had taken a bigger toll than the others knew of. It wouldn't be gone until his wings, legs, and even heart would give out. If there was to be anything left of it.

"My end begins here, Ish," Hericore heaved a tired sigh as he addressed the corpse beside him. "A story of woe and waning wills. All beginning with my stone soul."

-Fin-

<u>Special Thanks</u>

This project wouldn't have been possible without
the backing and support of some amazing
individuals. These special people are:

Alistair 'AJ' Martin

Danny Goldsmith

Eleanor Joyce

Genine

Henry Double

Holden Stenner

Mark Armstrong Allard

Maureen Robinson

Michael Grover

Pat Barker

Steph Sayer

"The Twins" Tracy and Wendy

Appendix

The Paladin's Order of Vitality:

–Hericore, Arch-Paladin, head of the Order's High
Council

–Philip, Hericore's ward and mailman in the Order

–Zarpadon, the fallen angel and Hericore's personal
assistant

–Krell, servant of Hericore

–Percival Hart, Warden of Refracted Light Prison

–Commander Lux, higher up in Valordolt's city watch

The Prisoners:

–Kenneth Porter, Central Block prisoner

–Donsis Allisteel, felony escaping the law, loan shark
notorious across the land

Other Characters:

–Ish, clockmaker living in Valordolt, creator of Sicilla

–Sicilla, mechanical daughter of Ish, an adventurer
allied with members of the Order

–Kalsec, young and mysterious crook wielding a
powerful weapon both inside and out

–Syphus, masked weapons collector and spymaster
from the Arcwoods

–Alva, Kalsec's ward and master of the dark arts

–'Zero', decrepit resident of the retirement home

Gods of Prime:

–Bethany the Blessed, Goddess of Life, daughter of
Gideon and Valentine

–Aldrich the Forsaken, God of Undeath, son of Gideon
and Valentine

–Solaris, God of the Sun, banished

–Luna, Goddess of the Moon, sister to Solaris

Locations:

–Magnus, land of mortals

–Midgartt, central continent of Magnus

–Vitalands, land of the Order, located in west Midgartt

–Valordolt, capital of the Vitalands

–Betiel, city in the Vitalands

–Igial's Lane, Hamlet in the Vitalands

–Casterlands, land of the Caster Council, located in east
Midgartt

–Arcwoods, land of the Birch Dynasty, located in north Midgartt

–Wasternlands, the western continent of Magnus

–Prime, land of the gods

–Etheriam, the waters of heaven

–Tarus, the heated pits of hell

Items of Importance:

–Arcane Magic, magic drawn from living thing

–Ethereal Magic, magic drawn from the dead or stagnate

–Necrotic Magic, magic stuck between Arcane and Ethereal forms, an undead state of magic

–Dark Magic, a mixture of all three main magic forms

–Arc-Mech, short for 'Arcane Mechanica,' a constructed race of machine lifeforms

–Quartz Lock, a special device that can alter time

–Pyrus, an elemental crystal of condensed heat energy

–Cryus, an elemental crystal of condensed ice